# CENTRIFUGAL
## Unstories by
## MATTHEW BURNSIDE

*Whisk(e)y Tit*
*VT & NYC*

Acknowledgments

With gratitude to the following venues for giving my work a home: Starskins is forthcoming in Hobart, Caustics: A Love Story is forthcoming in Always Crashing, The Prognosticators appeared in Okay Donkey, Digital Dreaming and Dear Wolfmother appeared in Heavy Feather Review, Pan's Lobotomy appeared in State of Imagination, Procession of the Dogface Lepers appeared in Gloom Cupboard.


Anti-Acknowledgments

With equal but opposite derision, disdain, and scorn for: entropy, negentropy, and paper cuts.

It seemed like a mistake. And mistakes ought to be rectified, only this one couldn't be. Between the way things used to be and the way they were now was a void that couldn't be crossed. I had to find an explanation other than the real one, which was that we were no more immune to misfortune than anybody else, and the idea that kept recurring to me...was that I had inadvertently walked through a door that I shouldn't have gone through and couldn't get back to the place I hadn't meant to leave.

–William Maxwell, *So Long, See You Tomorrow*

# REMNANTS

# STARSKINS

Dear Great & Yonder Silence,

Do you know how to leave this Earth? Because I really need to leave this Earth tonight. Jettison my skin. Supernova in a brilliant burst. I can feel my bones buckling beneath the weight of gravity and I cannot bear to be in such a boring place even one more night.

So I won't. Tonight is the night. Tonight, I blow this popsicle stand.

Await me in the far corner of the cosmos?

It isn't that life is bad so much as it's just not big enough for me. My mom reminds me of this every day, that I am such a strange girl. "Z, why can't you play with a regular doll instead of cutting up all the pretty ones you have and making them weird?"

That, and her boyfriend is so corny. Jeff smells like Dr. Pepper and Nicorette gum. His mustache is right out of a cartoon. At the movies he pours Raisinets into the popcorn bucket and orders a giant pickle, says That's the ticket! when the concession stand attendant hands it to him in a giant Dixie Cup. He cuts it in two, wraps one half in a napkin so he can eat it later that night as a bedtime snack. Days later, the smell is somehow still on him.

※

Mom also forbade me from listening to David Bowie but I listened to him anyway. At night, for years he lived inside my pillow. Sang me to sleep through tangled ear buds. I knew if I listened carefully I might just decode his secrets, the ones he had embedded into his songs for the true listeners. It finally happened. The solution to all my problems lay scattered in Life on Mars? :

♫ *It's a God-awful small affair | To the girl with the mousy hair* (that's me!) | *Now she walks through her sunken dream | To the seat with the clearest view | But the film is a saddening bore | For she's lived it ten times or more | She could spit in the eyes of fools | Sailors fighting in the dance hall* ♫

※

So I've built a spaceship out of a claw foot bathtub. It's filthy, so I wash it well first. Arrange my Space Army of Barbies, my trusty co-pilots, along the rim of the cold tub. There is: Bayonet Barbie, Chainsaw Slayer Barbie, Barbie Minotaur, Gamma Ray Barbie, Zombie Barbie, and finally, Shiva Barbie, Destroyer of Worlds.

Open the bathroom window, part the curtains, get ready. We belong in a wider sky, you and I. Prepare for blast off.

※

At first everything is so bright and quiet. All is paradise. But then I make the mistake of trying to count the stars.

There are no seahorses in outer space, either. I don't know why I thought there would be?

My bones have gone numb; they'll crumble soon enough like chalk in the celestial undertow. I've got a bad case of the helium knees and a bottomless void in my belly. I shiver all the time, my spine a rubber band in the quantum bend of space, my hands cold as porcelain.

Emptiness echoes here. There's nothing louder than loneliness.

Time works differently here, too. It's been a hundred eons and my body remains caught in a strange loop boomeranging through the beyond, an electric fog in which my consciousness is fixed yet my body is no longer childlike. I float, faster and faster, pinball of skin. There is only void. Occasionally I'll see the flash of a satellite but that's about it.

The universe is mostly vacant space. I guess that's why it's called space?

How could I miss the warnings, there in plain sight:

> ♫ *Far above the moon | Planet Earth is blue | And there's nothing I can do* ♫

I'm so sorry, mom. I would do anything to take it all back.

I even miss Jeff. His ridiculous mustache, finger guns and yes, even his pickle cologne.

I want to crash into your arms, be caught again. Drag me through every constellation—dust of a thousand worlds like shattered glass glittering. Crash me into the moon. Just deliver me home again.

To hell with eternities: just give me back my one good, lousy life.

✀

I need you to know, whoever is listening to this transmission there on the other side, if there even is a there anymore, that you are so much bigger than the smallness you've been made to suffer at the hands of the callous and the cruel. You are so tall, beautiful and brave and though this world may never contain you it is the only world you've got, so love it as you would love your one and only world. You are not the minor speck the universe has made you feel like you are. You are a billion specks, all luminous, limned with infinities. You contain so many precision-needlepoints of perfection, made of light and breath and bright things.

I know now no one will ever hear this, I have accepted my fate, but I'm beaming it out anyway. I've heard some radio waves can travel light years beyond their power's capacity, so I will do my best to dream it into being. To hope again and fire my message across an uncrossable ether. In my heart, it has already arrived. Bounced through eternity, skated along Saturn's rings, slingshot through oblivion.

It's too late for me but it's not too late for you. Yes, you. Listen: life is so very long and regret lasts forever. Whatever it is, whatever it is calling you away from this planet tonight, go back. Turn back now. Stay, because I promise you all the stupid little parts are the stupid little parts you'll miss most. I swear it, cross my heart and hope to die: Home is a thing you'll know once you've lost it.

Sincerely Yours,

Z for Zephyr

Centrifugal

# RELIQUARIES OF THE LOVELESS

Yes I died but not in the way that you think. There is no death like that, none so permanent. Only the temporary little spasms in passing from one form to the next. The truth that comes after the light is we're reborn in the shape of the thing we loved most during our life. Isn't that nice? I thought so too. Lucky for me, I became a book in a library. I won't tell you which book because that's my secret, nor will I tell you the library where I spend most of my days peering out through a spine to the passing perusers, wracked with their ruin or loneliness or love or imagination, fuses lit, waiting to be ignited. All that grisly business of being a human being, with which I am blessed to no longer be concerned. As a ghost in a book, I get to bear witness and watch and sometimes help by scratching something in the margins of my skin. Readers never know the words came from me, they just assume it's a leftover from other renters; it doesn't matter where the words come from, it's where they go and what they do next that matters. How they ensorcell a heart or ink a monochromatic dream into iridescent Technicolor.

*

Sometimes I whisper and no one arrives to pluck my spine, thumb through my tender pages. That's ok. I was hardly listened to in life, too, but who needs to be heard when there are so many rabbit holes of books to fall through?

Today I'm watching a young boy in the corner cubby desk. He's chewing on his bookmark, lost in worlds, full of futures. I see him every weekend. Watch him wave goodbye to his mom through the window. His friends are all playing baseball on a day like today but he chooses to be here instead. He is one of my favorites. His clothes are always dirty but his smile is always clean. He always appears on the verge of laughing, a nervous smirk that never quite cracks, except when one of my fellow books makes him cry. He never wants anyone to see him then, as if taught to be ashamed of his sadness. He waits patiently until the moment passes, last page speared with his pinkie, then with no-longer-glistening-eyes resumes his reading, wondering, daydreaming.

Only once has he touched me. He read me so fast he didn't even catch my message in the margins.

*You*
*Are*
*Seen.*

*

Books make great tear catchers; open up pretty much any book and just start weeping.

*

At night when there's nobody to watch I focus instead on the powerline through the window. Sometimes a bird will land there and I always worry it will get electrocuted, but this same brave little bird doesn't seem to share that fear. Sometimes, if the wind is blowing, he'll ride it like a rodeo bronco, wings bucking for balance until it's steady again. He could be dancing, for all I know.

*

Most books get a pretty good run, all things considered. Books like lives in miniature. Some are endowed with the finest covers and catchiest titles so they inhabit the front of the bookstore, airports and such. Known to all, they achieve fame and glory. Most get kicked to the bargain bin early on, but even then they can still end up here in the library and enjoy good long lives in relative obscurity. Some go unread entirely even when written with pure love. The saddest books are those that remain closed, collecting dust. I can hear them whimper sometimes.

The average paperback supposedly lives about 40 years, give or take.

Pages decay, grow brittle. Pictures yellow with the residue of age. Ink fades.

Time here is more fickle. Years blink by.

*

Today I'm watching a couple making out. Their shoulders brush against some of my neighbors, hearts thrumming as hands slip up thighs and tongues torque. This tends to happen more than you think in libraries. Silence can be very sexy. Plus, all that open space makes way for forbidden thoughts.

I miss having a body sometimes. I wish I had been kissed. It is at times like this I understand why the bird lands on the powerline. I fathom flight, velocity, voltage. Imagine a sky bleeding so many birds.

I leave a memo for the horny couple whose hands rake me off onto the carpet by accident, staring up splayed open:

*Please*
*Use*
*Protection.*

*

If you were to scan a parchment for various pigments you'd find a healthy mix of tears, sweat, and paper cuts inflicted by some poor author suffering from the delusion that, if only they arrange the words in exactly the right order, they too will be made immortal. But this isn't how it works, not quite. Books that live in the author's head alone are only half alive. It isn't until they're read truly by one other reader that they are brought to life. Only then can they live forever. Only then can they be reborn, like me.

A dreamless world need dreamers.

*

Then one day I am watching someone whose heart has been crushed. I know because she is one half of the couple, weeping where they once made love.

I leap off the shelf, this time on my own volition. Etch a pick-me-up.

*It's*
*His*
*Loss.*

*

My advice? Bury yourself into someone's heart. If you're meant to be there their roots will welcome you home. If not, they will spurn you. This violence will hurt every single time, I won't lie, but you will survive to swim back to the surface eventually. But you must try. You must get lost to get found; must die to dive. Waste your ache while you can. Squander your savage love. What the hell is a living for otherwise?

Well. Go on, then...                    The dreamless world awaits.

*Bleed*

*Brave*

*Birds.*

Centrifugal

Matthew Burnside

# TRANSMIGRATION OF THE SOUL: A CHEAT SHEET

As you know "The Big Test" is coming up soon. Commensurate with the Department of Transmigration's guidelines <u>one official cheat sheet is permitted per passenger</u>, as much as can be fitted onto one page. All results final. No calculators allowed.

---

Vocabulary: *Spectral Escort* – Though you must undertake this next step alone the journey need not necessarily be lonely, as upon slipping through the Extramundane Folds onto the Supernal Plane you will be greeted by your most beloved pet from your lifetime to help usher you onto the next phase, except this time they can talk! Their voice will sound exactly as you imagined. *The Numinous Leap* – Remember that this journey is a process, one that can prove taxing and arduous even to the most seasoned and well-tempered of repeat passengers. For this reason, you are encouraged to proceed at your own pace. Before taking the numinous leap, feel free to convalesce in your favorite place from life as if it were your very own bed & breakfast – whether real or imagined, fictive or not. When your heart is ready, a shimmering door will appear. *Secondskin* – the second you shed your mortal skin you will instantly assume your true form, the you you have been all along, beyond sense, beyond sight, imperceptible to the mortal eye with all its innumerable deceptions, tricks, grifts, and judgments. *Orphic Gift* – You will be privy to one – no more, no less – arcane secret or item of cosmological knowledge that was otherwise unknowable to you until the moment of your transmigration... Want to know if aliens exist? Who killed JFK? What really happened on February 7th, 1983 when you were just entering your 117th cycle? No problem! *Travel Relic* – Where you're going you won't require any luggage, no toiletries or trappings of luxury, but until you've learned to let go of all material attachments you may retain in your possession one earthly keepsake, a favored memento from your time here... Teddy bear, wedding ring, the baseball bat you used to hit that grand slam in 9th grade where your dad was present, who was so proud, etc. *Reckoning* – Definitely not obligatory, but if you are so inclined to revisit the moment you most regretted in your life, or a memory you hate you may... it's totally up to you, of course, however it is important to understand nothing you do will ever alter this moment, even in the imagination, for without it you wouldn't be you. Where you go next, these kinds of remainders are to be jettisoned to make room for building a new soul, but if it helps you are encouraged to revisit one last time if only to learn to let it go, finally. *Miraculous Tax* – we like to leave passengers with a little taste of what their absence is making possible so all passengers, before disembarking, will be treated to a vision of the nearest miracle in proximity—a child being born, a couple falling in love, an act of pure kindness, all afforded by the timely donation of your Extramundane Matter (see #2 in Equations & Formulas). *Sigils & Spirals* – You may experience novel colors and impossible textures upon transmigration. This is completely normal and no cause for panic! *Museum of the Elsewhat* – Another prodigious perk compliments of the Divine Everafter Fund, all passengers may delight in the amenities and exhibits of one of our many Museums of the Elsewhat, where itinerant travelers may enjoy designing their very own animal to inhabit the next world to come (how do you think the walrus came about?), reading about their previous cycles in our OmniLibrary of Eternium, venturing through an antique time or unarrived future in the Flux Blender, or redefining physics in one of our many terrestrial crafting stations. *Rumination Windfall* – Leave some inspiration, unfulfilled vision, or residual daydream behind for someone else by joining our Dedicated Muses Program. *The Big Cleanse* – Somewhat intense, experience the ecstatic pain of mankind one last time by swimming through the tears of the universe in our dedicated Weeping Pool. *Infinity's Jukebox* – On the way out, all passengers will hear their favorite song as if for the first time, made anew, as you will soon be made anew.

Equations & Formulas:   #1) $\Delta U = Q$   #2) Entropy $= S$   #3) Lemniscate $= \infty$   #4) $E = mc2$   #5) $e^{\wedge}(i\pi)+1=0$

Possible Essay Topics: "What was your favorite thing?" + "What was the point of all this?" + "Any complaints, suggestions for our customer service department?"

---

## FAQs:

**Will it hurt?**   No more than plucking a splinter, or shard of glass, from your open palm. Except this shard, once removed, will be the most beautiful shard of glass you've ever seen— one that blooms backwards into a beach, into a sea, into all islands ever; Into space, the stars; Into every winking light and somnolent shadow.

**Should I be scared?** Someone like you? No. Fear is only for the living. Here, it is as useless as currency.

**What about everyone else?** You will see them again soon, we promise; there are no parallel lines in this dimension... all paths converge again eventually.

**Can I go in someone else's place or vice versa?** Such switches are sometimes permissible with pre-approval.

**What if I'm not ready to go? Did I fail?** Very few aren't even when they think they are. And no, you didn't fail because there is no failure. You're just not finished. A completed soul can take hundreds of cycles before it's done "cooking". The path there is meandering and at times tedious. We ask for your patience.

**What is the shape of the universe?** Love is a spiral you fall into, sky without zenith that never tires of catching you. Hate, a hole only hungry for more holes.

**Where is God in all this & may I meet Him?** SHE occasionally takes appointments but never in Her true form, which would obliterate you.

**What if I want to go back?** You can, but only when you're ready to return and the world is ready to receive you. Until then, be grateful forever hasn't yet arrived.

Centrifugal

# THE PROGNOSTICATORS

It occurred to all of us about the same time that our little brother could see the truth at the bottom of the well: how all fates entwined triple-knotted gleaming in their misery, held together by a wise but stubborn old snake named Mister Misty McRattly Tail, Esquire.

In those days we took turns dangling him by his dusk-colored ankles when we weren't busy picking at scabs on the porch, or catching too-low clouds scudding overhead toward a big pink horizon of demise.

While it was my turn my sister Witch Hazel counted her splinters gleefully while Buck Owens tore apart a rocking chair and Salinger packed an ant pile into an old pie tin. "Look how big the peppercorns panic!" he hooly-hawed, before pouring it down the back of Zipperboy's overalls.

"What's baby see now?" yelled one of em again. I don't know which. "Getting closer" I reported, lowering the rope cinched round baby's ankles as he giggled furiously into the void. "Good baby. Go go go!"

The game of it was *just so*: Noose up thine soft baby ankles and let descend. Get baby close enough to catch snake in mouth. Pull up for a prize. Most days it wasn't about winning—just giving a name to our madness.

Soda bottle chimes clanked together strung from their limbs now. An owl peered out from a knothole. "What's baby see?"

"Not quite yet" I reported, feeling sludgeblooded and starved for action. "First one to brick a bird gets to pet the spider!" one of em announced. I don't know which.

Next thing I know the sky is thick with salmon dust and breathing is a chore. "Cut it" a neighbor hollered. They must had been burning; I could smell it in the air. Disinfected suds and gristle.

Then all were out wide in the yard equidistantly posed: one burning up the kiddy pool, one blowing black bubbles, one pinching mushrooms, one picking for nose coal. Deep diving.

"What's baby see?"

"Almost almost," I reported. Flung my attention down the hole and heard a rising whistle. Like fishhooks swirling around in a bowl made of molars. Glass clicking through its crooked lips.

Someone yodeled. Another yelled out a word we were taught never to say aloud.

Everyone fell down at once, crashing through the grass itch-riddled and red.

"What's baby see?"

"Nigh coming up" I reported, feeling a sugar high. Sudden summer heat in my bones.

I could feel the future rumbling in my belly, like that pie tin full of ants. Could taste time and rain backwards. Throat full of dandelion parade...little baby bulbs and serpent skulls.

Giddy and sad without knowing or caring to know the extent of my own edges.

"What are you children up to now?" said Mother, summoning us for dinner.

Inside, we dunked our heads, said grace, scraped our plates clean.

"So—" Father finally said, slurping his canteen. "How was your day?" In the distance hills were hiccupping; sirens sloshed around like wild bells drunk on panic. Our sheepheads tilted as night was coming on strong, guttering through the slanted board. Mother gnawed a cactus in the disposal.

"Everything is wonderful" I said as baby wriggled, laughing through the snake writhing round in its gummy maw. "Why do you ask?"

Centrifugal

# **RENDEZVOUS**

We were all in such a damn hurry to arrive at exactly the same destination with exactly the same mileage, though some of us took shortcuts and some of us took the long way around, and those of us in denial that the end was coming found the trip strangely shorter while those of us who had accepted its inevitability found it longer than expected, which was both fair and unfair, and while we all initially feared the cost of the toll crossing the bridge, what we came to realize is what we actually feared was the startling lack of assurances that we would ever see each other on these same roads again, or any road at all for that matter, at any speed, in any town, a passing blur in the halo of a headlight, and, in fact, we were already pre-missing each other long before we had even parted.

Centrifugal

# PUNCTUM

About 6,530,000 results (0.44 seconds)

Dictionary

Search for a word     🔍

🔊 **punc·tum**
/ˈpəNGktəm/

*noun*   TECHNICAL

a small, distinct point.
- ANATOMY
  the opening of a tear duct.

1. I've always had an affinity for sharp things even if I've never been one. I once read in a book, WE REAP NOT WHAT WE BLEED BUT WHAT WE ALLOW TO BE BLED. Moments later I got a paper cut, dripped a page completely red, soaked to the skin, closed it up, and put it back on the shelf without ever saying a word about it.

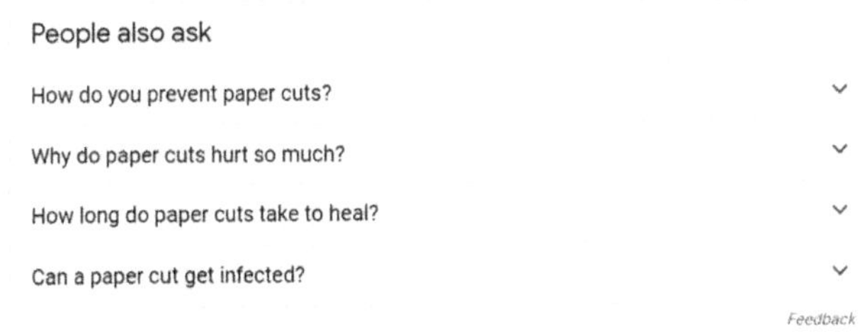

People also ask

How do you prevent paper cuts?   ⌄

Why do paper cuts hurt so much?   ⌄

How long do paper cuts take to heal?   ⌄

Can a paper cut get infected?   ⌄

Feedback

2. This is a brief history of things that cut.

Things to do in Marfa Fucking Texas     ✕   🎤   🔍

🔍 All    🖾 Images    ◎ Maps    ▸ Videos    🗉 News    ⋮ More      Settings    Tools

3. Where I'm from, we have a mannequin factory. Sometimes I sneak in and saw the heads off dummies. Stick em on cactuses to ward off the wild boars. Other times I'll sneak into half-built houses and throw kitchen knives at the wall, even though they never stick. Kitchen knives aren't meant for that sort of thing. A knife is a knife is a knife, I figure. One day I'll get em to stick.

About 10,100,000 results (0.42 seconds)

: a villainous son of Poseidon in Greek mythology who forces travelers to fit into his bed by stretching their bodies or cutting off their legs.

www.merriam-webster.com › dictionary › Procrustes

Procrustes | Definition of Procrustes by Merriam-Webster

About featured snippets     Feedback

4. Listening to _____ in the grocery store at midnight hunting for fruit again, dreaming of cutting into every piece, the spray of their juice on my leather jacket and sunglasses while hoping somebody's cart crashes into me, where _____ = a) Depeche Mode b) Joy Division c) Prince d) New Order

Joy division love will tear us apart lyrics     ✕   🎤   🔍

5. Here in this place there's not much else to do but stargaze, look stuff up on the internet, watch movies. The old man is partial to cartoons. I, on the other hand, am partial to horror. The infamous heart-removing scene from Temple of Doom is one of my go-to scenes. No drip, no fuss, just one hand scooping out a meaty wad of organic valves, leaving the chest a vacant space, leaving some room to breath. The man is left both alive and unalive, miraculously. Only then is he worthy of sacrifice.

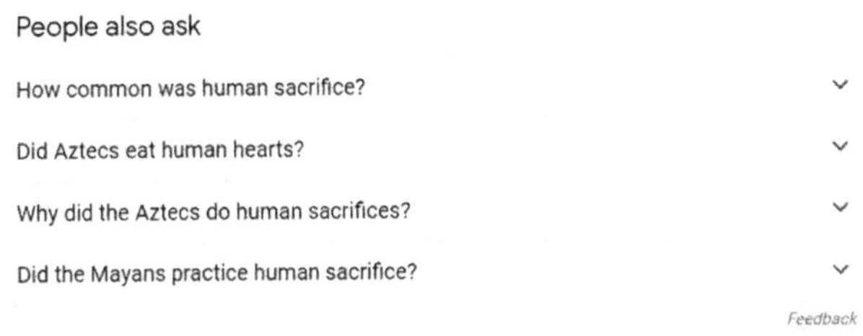



6. Some other movie scenes with which I've had unhealthy fascinations over the years: the barbwire room from Suspiria; needle haystack diving, Saw 2; Edward Scissorhands; Audition, Antichrist, The Hills Have Eyes; all the classics, pretty much every goreporn flick ever.

These aren't just movies—they're study guides.



7. What do you think would hurt more? a) kicking a wall with a toothpick fixed between your toenail b) a paper cut on your tongue c) barb wire pulled taut around your chest d) a bee sting on the eyeball?

8. In my least favorite version of Little Red Riding Hood, a cat actually says, "A slut is she who eats the flesh and drinks the blood of her grandmother!" This version is a tragedy.

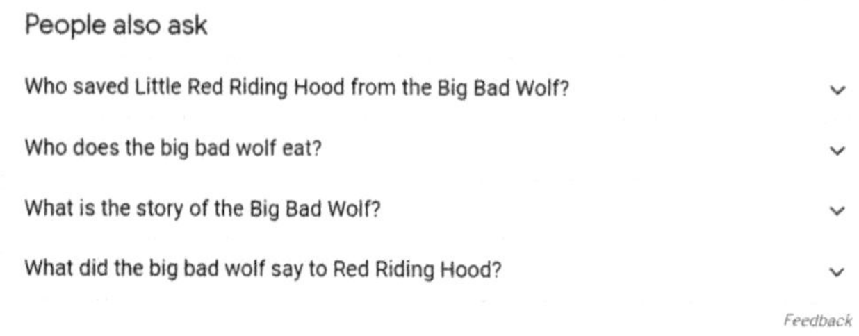



9. "See all these stars? They smile for you, my dear." Through his wooly mustache, a smoke-colored tusk, he speaks. "How can you learn without being taught? How else are you supposed to know it's love if it doesn't hurt?"

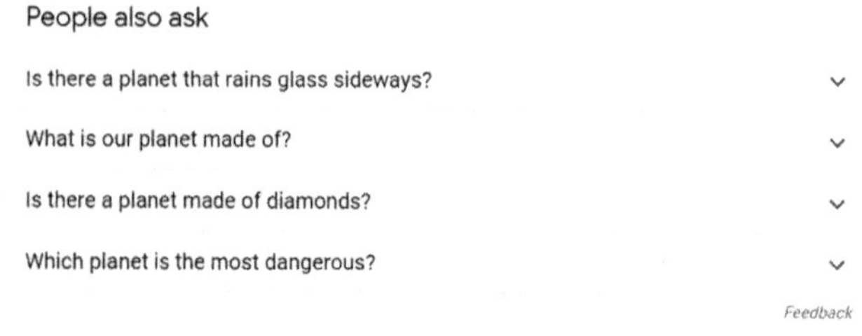



10. So one day you buy a bus ticket out of town. You imagine one of those ACME saws cutting a circle out of the blackness. Stick a leg in to test the waters. Falling through it is much harder. You tuck the ticket away in your back pocket, watch the bus go by. Sun sets, stars sparkle. Satellite dishes beam their silence into space from the desert.

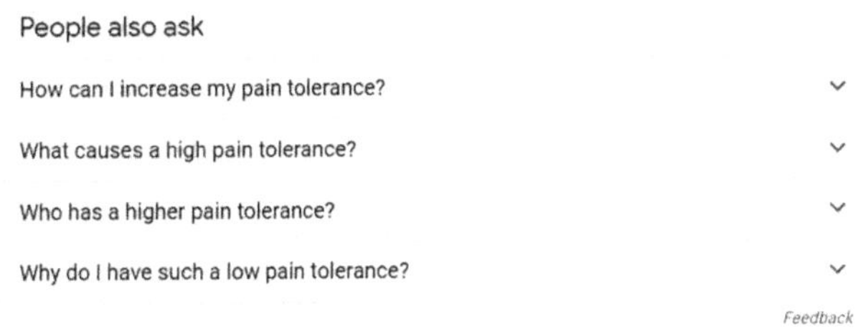


11. I'm told I have an excellently high threshold for pain. It's become a point of pride but not by choice.

People also ask

How can I increase my pain tolerance?

What causes a high pain tolerance?

Who has a higher pain tolerance?

Why do I have such a low pain tolerance?

*Feedback*

12. The American desert, as depicted in Looney Tunes by illustrator Maurice Noble, is a majestic, romanticized, idealized version. In reality there's very little to love. The desert here is long, seemingly inescapable. I wish I could fold the stars into my pocket, feel them pulsing against my thighs, triangulate their warmth and focus them into a laser beam to redirect toward my enemies. If I could be any ACME product, I'd probably be Invisible Paint.

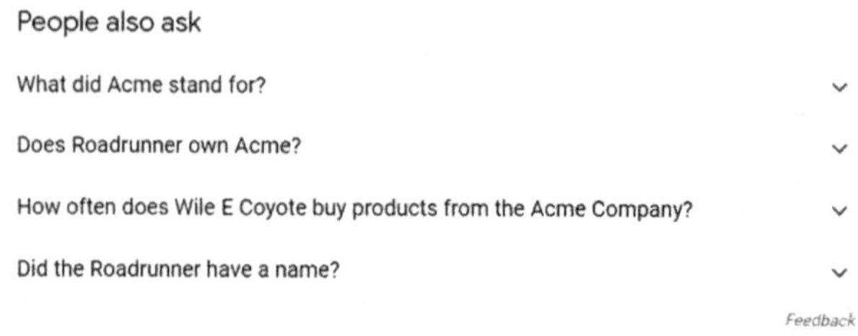


13. In another version, it is the gentle wolves who are most dangerous of all. The kind who wave to everyone downtown, tip well, attend church, read bedtime stories, even show you how to identity stars through a telescope. This version is a cautionary tale.

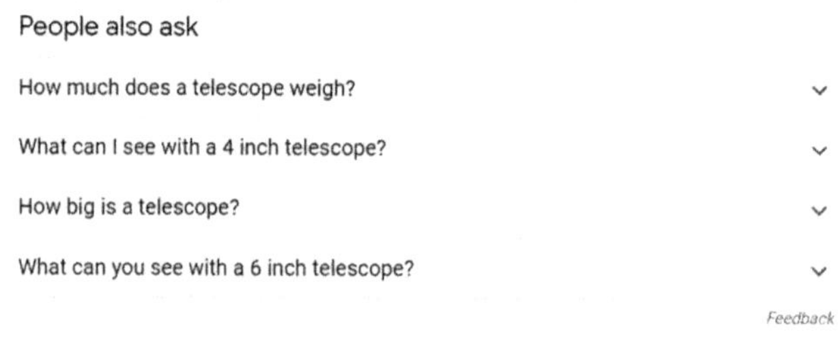


14. I always hated Happily Ever After. Not that it doesn't come, it does, but what's the use of something that arrives so late? By then, the damage is already done.

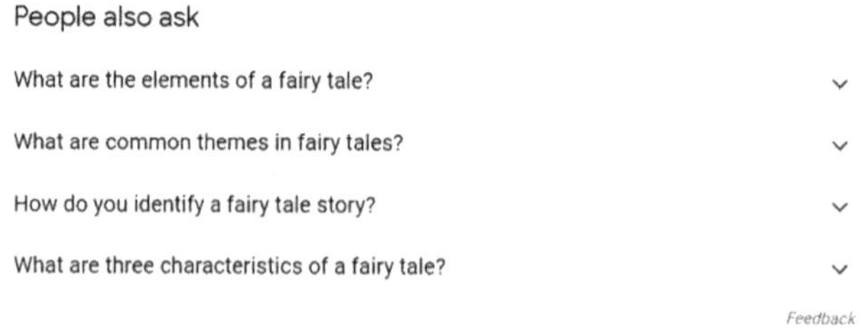

15. I've tried reading long meandering novels, the kind that ramble on and on for hundreds and hundreds of pages with their prologues and epiphanies and yadda yadda, but few keep my attention or even resemble a reality I'm familiar with, unless the sentences really cut but even then I get bored. You read and you read and read, all the while you're searching for the heart of the thing, scrambling for some shred of decent plot, conflict, closure to wring any iota of order out of the soul-sucking chaos-sponge that is a life. But what if there is none? What if true life is plotless? What if the heart IS the heart and the only prevailing logic a sawtooth desire to brand your pain, which is inescapable, like the desert, into a shape that you can call your own and not his? Anybody's, I mean.

16. Out of all the constellations I think Orion, the hunter, is my favorite, as is his fate at the hands of Artemis.

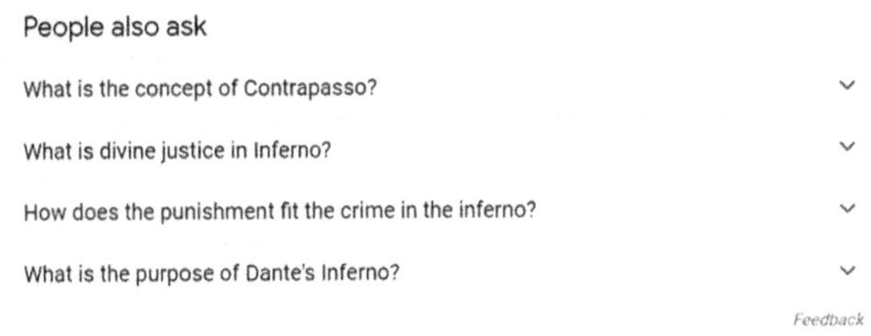



17. Dreamed of butterflies with butterfly knives for wings again last night.

18. What do you think would hurt more? a) being alone forever b) being with someone who makes you feel alone c) being raised by someone who makes you feel like you deserve to be all alone d) all of the above.

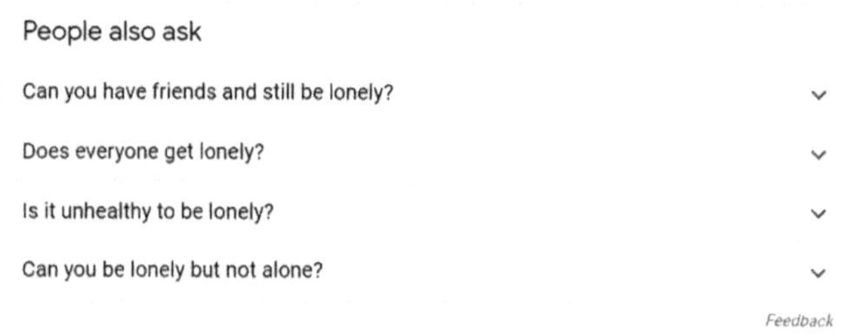



19. Do you believe you deserve to be happy? a) yes b) no c) maybe d) ask me again later.

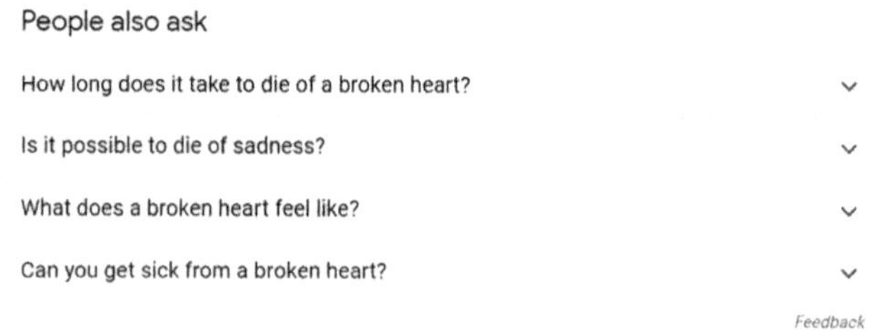



20. Two scenes from Home Alone also come to mind: the one where Marv pops glass ornaments under his bare feet stepping

inside a window and the other, a tar nail through the foot. I must've rewound those on my VHS tape a thousand times. Wasn't a sexual thing, but it was a source of visceral pleasure, an aesthetic appeal. At its heart, Home Alone is a revenge fantasy. Kevin McCallister is a bloodthirsty hunter extracting divine retribution for something unforgivable. It's not the wet bandits who are to blame, even though they receive the brunt of his vengeance. I don't blame him. After all, how can you forget a whole entire child on Christmas?

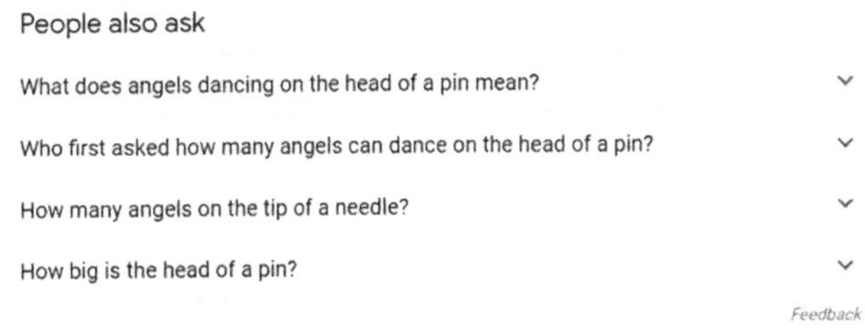

People also ask

What does angels dancing on the head of a pin mean?

Who first asked how many angels can dance on the head of a pin?

How many angels on the tip of a needle?

How big is the head of a pin?

*Feedback*

21. You internalize at some point negative attention is at least better than no attention at all. Better than neglect. Something is better nothing, right? A cactus is better than emptiness.

New order age of consent lyrics

22. Not by the hair of my chinny chin chin! said the little piggie to the wolf, knowing all the while one day the roles would be reversed.

How to spear a pig

23. The thing about the desert here is the ground is so dry it cracks everywhere. Shovels can't get their teeth down in the scrub without breaking.

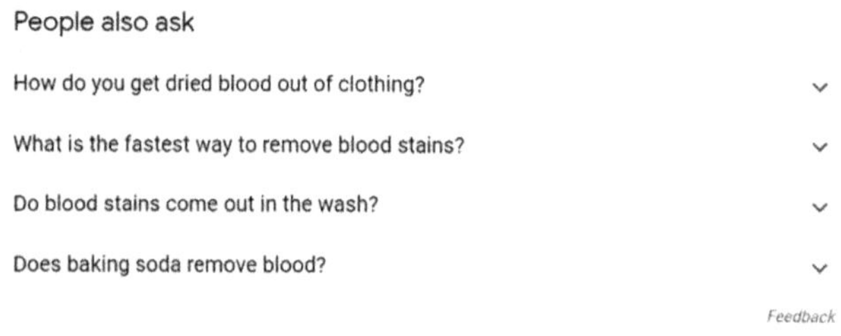


24. In my almost-favorite version, a hunter comes along and cuts Little Hood from the wolf's belly with a pair of scissors. This version is a comedy.



25. You can learn anything from the internet. For example, did you know that the fracture threshold of the human skull is anywhere from about 14.0 to 68.5 Joules? Did you also know a polish brass telescope with collapsible mahogany tripod is more than capable of administering that kind of blunt force, though it helps to render the recipient of said force immobile first? A few pokes with any sharply-edged implement should do the trick.

I've always been self-taught—a quick and efficient understudy.

How else can you learn without being taught?

People also ask

What is the best bait for wild hogs?

How long does it take for wild hogs to find bait?

What food attracts wild boar?

How do you trap a wild boar?

*Feedback*

26. So one day you feed one pig's heart to another pig.

People also ask

How are pigs and humans different?

Can a pig's heart be used in humans?

Which animal heart is closest to human?

Are pigs anatomically similar to humans?

*Feedback*

27. In my favorite as yet unwritten version, Little Red Riding Hood gets the fuck out of the forest. She finds a new place where red can symbolize something other than blood. She has always been sharp, not dull as the wolf would have her believe. The stars don't just smile for her, they tremble. This version is neither comedy nor tragedy—it exists in a third dramatic Shakespearean category called, simply, history.

People also ask

How do I find my best smile?

How can I train myself to smile?

How can I smile without looking awkward?

How do I make myself smile again?

*Feedback*

28. You can't have New Order without Joy Division.

New order ceremony lyrics

29. "Show me your heart. Go ahead: Cut it out. Remove it. Do it now, do it slow. Place it in my hands, an icky offering..."

**People also ask**

What does that's all folks mean?

Did Bugs Bunny say that's all folks?

Who said thats all folks?

Who first said that's all folks?

*Feedback*

30. "... How else are you supposed to know it's love if it doesn't hurt?"

**People also ask**

How much is a Greyhound bus ticket to Dallas Texas?

How much is a bus ticket to Dallas?

How much is a bus ticket to Texas?

Does Megabus go to Dallas Texas?

*Feedback*

31. Somewhere in Marfa, Texas, a cactus smiles.

what if my mouth hurts from smiling too much

32. It smiles for you, my dear.

and they lived happily ever after

33. There are eighty-eight officially recognized constellations; out of those eighty-eight, sixty-six have violent mythologies associated with them; out of those sixty-six, thirty-three are lethal figures.

Fatal really, not to be tampered with.

On a clear night like tonight, you can see them all.

**You Are Not Connected to the Internet**

This page can't be displayed because your computer is currently offline.

Centrifugal

# ~~NO EXIT: A GALLERY OF EXISTENTIAL HORRORS~~

///

*Smooth and smiling faces everywhere, but ruin in their eyes.*

*Everything has been figured out, except how to live.*

—Jean-Paul Sartre

///

[Roll D20]

## Scenario #0

The numinous zero, as we know it today, wasn't invented until 628 CE. Medieval Christians feared it for what it represented—The Void, and so forbade it from use, only daring to use it in secret. It stands alone as both a number and non-number, containing both thereness and not-thereness. The ability to conceive of this abstraction is one of the things that sets humans apart from the rest of the animal kingdom. Even bees, quite intelligent, cannot fathom the symbolic import of the numeral that both is and is not. A misbehaving anomaly as ridiculous as a nautilus swimming through the eye of a needle, the zero insists on persisting despite its inherent implausibility, in all its glorious itness.

## Scenario #1

A committee of your former lovers sits gathered downstairs in your living room. You can't quite understand what they're deliberating with such vigor—the shape of your demise, fate of your soul, future love lives and beyond? Only one of them seems sympathetic, despite all the things you once put them through. "It is time," says the chairperson, most brokenhearted of the bunch. "Bring them down."

## Scenario #2

You slip out of a work party to be alone. Sneak a smoke on the curb, flick your lighter at the moon. But there are people gathered there so you move further down the block into an alley where another party has gathered formed of people who have escaped their own respective parties. To escape this party, you slip into a partially opened garage, try to duck out only to find more people, an escape party of escapees from the party away from the original party. Everywhere you go: the scaffolding of a house under construction, dank sewers, atop the old water tower, even a cave festooned with drippy stalactites at the edge of the woods, you encounter only more faces with the same pair of unblinking, sparkless eyes. *(People, people, everywhere, And all the crowds did slink / People, people, everywhere, Nor any place to think.)*

## Scenario #3

Futurity is a flower bracing to be torn apart, petals shattered by the storm. It is not the storm that wilts it but the knowledge that a storm is coming, and because of this its beautiful thorns grow dull. Because of this, it learns to hate the sun.

## Scenario #4

*Apeirophobia*—terror of eternity. Healthy fear of foreverness and the unbroken ∞, also known as a lemniscate. Most are haunted by the inevitably of death but for many the opposite scenario is equally haunting. Conceptually impossible to hold in one's head, the idea of infinity has been known to drive many a man mad...

## Scenario #5

In The Artist of the Beautiful by Nathaniel Hawthorne, a blacksmith obsessed with perpetual motion builds a clockwork butterfly, his masterpiece, only to find it ironically crushed in the palm of his hand by story's end. So many nights spent toiling in his shop by dim lamplight, how many times he must have glimpsed out the window at the passersby laughing at the futility of his craft's end. I wonder, did he ever see behind them to the blooming cherries and night-birds and swaying boughs. Did he ever ask, is it the tree moving or is it the wind or is it my mind moving them both?

Let it go, Owen Warland, I want to yell at him.

There is no catching the fucking butterfly.

All is bejeweled wreckage.

But I can't yell at him because he's just a character in a story and I am just a reader.

I will never touch or know him just as he will never touch or know the butterfly.

It is all a mercy.

## Scenario #6

The production is on fire. The curtains are on fire. The set, painted backdrop, cut-out moon, stenciled stars: all on fire. The actors, saying their lines through on-fire throats, enunciate on fire because the dialogue is on fire and the script is on fire. The director, backstage building a birdhouse because the sky is on fire, is on fire. The writer at home on opening night because no one bothered to invite him is sleeping in his bed on fire. His dreams are on fire. If he had been invited, his tickets would have arrived in an envelope on fire. The audience sitting in their fiery chairs applaud through fiery digits. eyes on fire. They witness art that is on fire, because the continuous dream is on fire. The smoke, the fumes, atoms and molecules, all on fire. The fire on fire. Life is on fire, so you might as well burn brightly.

## Scenario #7

Some other déjàs and vus...

*Jamais vu* = feeling of experiencing something anew even after that experience has occurred multiple times.

*Presque vu* = feeling of being on the verge of a realization that never arrives.

*Déjà rêvé* = feeling of having previously dreamed something you are currently experiencing.

*Déjà entendu* = feeling of having heard something that may only have been imagined.

## Scenario #8

As 70% of the Earth's surface is covered in water and considering the ocean's average depth is 12,400 feet and light can only carry through about 330 feet, it stands to reason that a majority of our planet is constantly covered in darkness all the time.

## Scenario #9

Repeat after me: Cat. Cat. Cat. Cat. Cat. Cat. Cat. Cat. Cat. Cat. (Repeat now 30 more times.) Eventually that word will begin to lapse into nonsense and even more, it will begin to lose all essence. This is what's known as Semantic Satiation, an apt demonstration of the human brain's ability to get bored with something and forget to attribute meaning to it. A similar phenomenon occurs with smells—if you've ever found yourself in a smelly place but unable to detect odors after a while, that's because your brain has stopped receiving messages from your olfactory receptors. Your tongue has stopped tasting itself. Your brain has essentially edited out your nose. If it can do all that, just imagine what other tricks it might be pulling.

## Scenario #10

A song you heard exactly once in a crowded bar, its drunken melody slightly out of sync, is fated to remain irrecoverable. Infinity's jukebox has no coin slots. All you will ever know is it is a song that is unknowable to you, as is the person you were when you heard it, as are the ears with which you never quite heard it and the hands though which that moment slipped. Little sand of the hours. They are not the same hands as your hands now. Your heart then is not the same timebomb ticking toward its extinction within your chest now. Gone, long gone are the moments! This one as well, gone now too, and this sentence, which will never be read by quite the same you again.

Is it knowing these moments and all these yous are lost forever that makes the sadness come, or is it the knowing about their unknowableness? How can you recover what was never lost? How can you remember what was never forgotten?

## Scenario #11

To further compound the phantasmagorical problems of #4 and #10, there are different kinds of infinities, according to Georg Cantor: Infinities that can be counted and infinities that can't be counted. Paradoxes and meta-paradoxes. The sphericalness of the color blue, for example, or the circumference of a tunnel dreaming in July.

## Scenario #12

Wittgenstein preferred language games, but he might have delighted in board games too. No doubt he would agree that no board game could truly epitomize the game of consciousness, however, with all its subliminal subterfuge. Only, perhaps, a sawed-apart-and-hot-glued-back-together-again Frankenstein version of several board games might could come even close—part Chess, part Monopoly, part Clue, part Twister, part Mouse Trap.

Snakes and Ladders, however, would not be included as it comes too close to reality.

## Scenario #13

A partial list of impossible geographies: the 10,000-year cuckoo clock inside the Sierra Diablo mountains in Texas whose cuckoo only emerges once in a millennium; The Uncanny Valley, which isn't a place at all but rather the feeling of unease or repulsion elicited by an artificial intelligence exhibiting remarkable human-like qualities. (While the scientific cause of this phenomenon isn't known, a few theories have been proposed: 1) we automatically differentiate such automatons as poor mates; 2) they trigger in us an innate fear of death or reduction; 3) as 'soulless beings' they represent a direct threat to human concepts of individuality, identity, and specialness); The Fairy Castle, an 8-foot dollhouse commissioned by silent film actress Colleen Moore for around seven million dollars with diamond, emerald, and pearl chandeliers, over 2,000 miniatures, the smallest bible ever created, and hand-painted murals by Walt Disney; The Gates of Horn & Ivory, which represent entrances to two different dimensions, one a realm of the real and the other a realm of falsehoods, shadow, and superficiality. ("For two are the gates of shadowy dreams, and one is fashioned of horn and one of ivory. Those dreams that pass through the gate of sawn ivory deceive men, bringing words that find no fulfilment. But those that come forth through the gate of polished horn bring true issues to pass, when any mortal sees them" —Spoken by Penelope, *The Odyssey*)...it remains debatable, however, which realm encompasses the truer reality; Mojave Phone Booth, an isolated phone booth which stood in the middle of Mojave National Preserve in California from 1948 to 2000. This graffiti-laden unsuspecting landmark became something of a phenomenon in 1997, garnering internet fame and the attention of a man who camped at the booth for 32 days, claiming the Holy Spirit had guided him there to answer phone calls. He did as he was instructed, answering over 500 of them, many of them from an individual identifying himself as 'Sergeant Zeno from the Pentagon'; The Red Brick Road, whose spiral path is clearly visible in The Wizard of Oz winding outward alongside its more famous cousin, The Yellow Brick Road, leaving Munchkin Land; The Penrose Staircase; Ouroboros; Bach's endless Musical Offering; pretty much all works of M.C. Escher; Yayoi Kusama's Infinity Mirrors; Isamu Noguchi's Play Mountain; The interconnected pipe network of rabbit holes from Super Mario Bros; Umberto Eco's concept of Hyperreality; Gertrude Stein's Tender Buttons; Kafka's bureaucratic labyrinths; finally, Anechoic Chambers—rooms so devoid of reverberation that one can hear their own blood flowing and the bones within their skin scraping, which goes to show: True silence screeches. Satellites tumble into oblivion and elsewheres abound. There are angels in outer space right now lopping each other in half, pantomiming eternities.

## Scenario #14

There is a rather distressing Kierkegaardian theory that posits we can never know whether we are or are not secretly doing the work of the devil. This applies to the highest saint down to the lowest sinner. That is, we can never truly know the rightness of our actions, the purity of our moral rectitude, even if we believe deep down these instincts come from a pure place.

We can only do as we do.

Play as we play.

## Scenario #15

Another night glazed with boredom - swirling in this velvet snowglobe of Am, confetti of consciousness churning - so you try hopping online, a smaller box within the small box of a room, but it only serves to elongate your loneliness. Is there anything left you haven't done? You set out to try something new: Saw a shadow in half. Put a match to a mirror, just to see if it will dance. Hold a piece of ice in your fist under hot water. Something about phase changes. Something about an equal but opposite action for every reaction. Something about all pain deriving from something else's pleasure, or vice versa. Something about bodies, too: this strange meat machine endowed with jiggling appendages, ligaments, belly buttons, kneecaps, necks, napes, and an alien mouth filled with teeth (what even ARE teeth?) and a tongue (what a concept!). Then, finally, something about why, if it's yours, you always feel like a tourist here?

## Scenario #16

One day you begin substituting the word Void into your favorite songs. Slipping it in for no particular reason.

*Let's Hear it for the Void...Paranoid Void...Everybody Wants to Rule the Void...*

Somewhere a secret song cartwheels through your subconscious, fluttering just behind your eyelids.

*Sympathy for the Void...Happiness is a Warm Void...Enjoy the Void....*

## Scenario #17

Memory begins under a tinkling piano. You are in the first grade with a classmate, she with her moo-cow skirt and pigtails, you with your overalls and perpetual cowlick. You are kissing, acting as if you both understand the act, behind a wall of neatly stacked salmon-colored bricks. Chapped lips smacking. Out of the window you spy a speckled chime made of soda bottles clanking impetuously and a power line you can just catch the corner of. Though it will be many years before you understand the meaning of voltage, you fathom for the first time how light and heat could come from the same exact source. How all eyes contain doors but only a few we get to walk through. You will coddle this memory many times, turning it over like a lucky coin in your pocket again and again, but nothing you do will ever put a name to the girl. Perhaps she remembers you similarly, but only the mere idea of you. You as a concept, a figment. Placeholder for memory's strange & cyclical loops.

Are we the things we remember or the things that remember us?

What about the things we choose not to remember?

All the things dearly misremembered?

Are we lost or found in our translations?

## Scenario #18

I don't know how else to say it: I don't know how to escape the artifice of art anymore. Another fatal existential quirk to be reckoned with. Call it fear of endings, like how instead of finishing a book sometimes I'll bury it so I never have to say goodbye. Never have to untether myself from imaginary people made of ink, somehow more real to me than some made of flesh that I've known.

Put another way, say I tell you a story? Say it is the story of how Buster Keaton, temporarily committed to an asylum for alcoholism, once escaped a straitjacket using a trick he had been taught by a childhood friend of the family named Harry Houdini.

Say it sounds too good to be true, so you refuse to research it further. To confirm nor deny its veracity by searching Wikipedia. Say you leave it there untouched so it will be true in the imagination. Say this is the truth that matters most.

## Scenario #19

Hope creeps in like a mushroom after the rain.

## Scenario #20

You were born to fall.

Maybe you have been falling all your life.

Diving down the page like avalanche. Like shimmering text, snowcrashing.

Some chasms are collected only by falling through them.

One day an author speaks to you through the page, through vessels of words, which are an empty container. They arrive uninvited. They arrive disconnectingly, maybe even disharmoniously. But maybe these words carry a weight nonetheless, with just enough force to pierce the distance, the illusion of distance, to prove their earnestness?

Perhaps they propel you, the reader, toward a somethingness?

*There is no winning or losing this game,* speaks the author through the artifice, willing you to listen before it's too late, which it always and never is. *There is only playing the game. So play.*

Matthew Burnside

Centrifugal

# MERCY KILLS

A man went in search of a tiger. He wanted to live. Years earlier food had begun to taste tasteless, his job lapsing into a series of jejune tasks, all love and lust for life having fled his heart. The tiger escaped from the zoo sometime around noon, so warbled the radio staticky through a tunnel as the man approached downtown. He had never met a wild animal before, only the domesticated sort, and even then stray cats never warmed to him, as if sniffing the strain of the pitiable upon him, turning their noses up at a free dish of tuna before bounding a wall or slipping between a loose slat of fence. The man wanted to meet something still wild because he thought he might siphon some of its spark. What were the chances of running into such a creature tonight: about the same as getting struck by lightning? The man craved electricity. His father had bequeathed to him on his thirteenth birthday a knife with a beautiful bone hilt, which he had never had occasion to use, afraid as he was of everything, a child trembling at every little shadow. Even still, every morning the man would sharpen his knife a little bit more. "Not sharp enough" he would reason at the end of each day; any excuse to keep the beast at bay. He remembered a movie he had seen as a kid featuring the act of seppuku, in which a samurai regained his lost honor. Hoisting his sword high, sun setting just over shoulder, the samurai plunged the blade into his belly, his final task complete. The man reckoned there would be no electricity for him. Some people were just born unlucky, he supposed. Popping the trunk he dug the knife out from within a blanket in which it was swaddled and shoved it inside his trench coat, curved his collar up at the night which was coming on, moon leering meanly down over the tightrope of a power line. You are going to be a great man, his father promised. But what if I'm not? I'm so scared of the world. Nonsense, said the elder, placing the knife into his hand. You must live each day like your first and last day on Earth. Of course it is so... why would I lie to you?

*

A tiger went in search of a man. He wanted to live. Years earlier he had been captured in the Sundarbans by hunters and taken far away from his family. He could still feel the swaying of the ship and the sloshing of the waves, jostled within his filthy cage as men stinking of tobacco clouds laughed gathered around a big poker table. The tiger wanted to meet a man. Call it simple revenge. One human life was as good as any other, because they were all shameful creatures. He had never met one worthy of sacrifice. In fact, no human had ever deigned to face him. Back home, they would resort to dirty tricks: wearing masks on the back of their heads and electrifying manakins—trick men with tricks in their eyes and tricks in their hearts—or hunting in groups as to overpower the mighty tiger. Not a single one had ever turned to lock eyes as one should facing a foe of equal but opposite courage in battle. Not one of them could be called a true warrior. When he finally reached his new home, the first thing the zoo did was have him declawed so he would lose his appetite for hunting. But in his dreams he hunted often, chasing his prey through a labyrinth of bricks and, being of a very clever kind, the tiger quickly formulated a plan to make his leave and have one final hunt. Every morning he would sharpen his claws a little more. "Not sharp enough" he would reason at the end of each day until one day they were, allowing him to scale the wall of his fake jungle. Looking at the towers around him the tiger had never felt larger; the moon smiled on, flashing its fangs, flinging stars thick-spattered across the sky. He could taste the first lie of the first hunter in his mouth now, the one who had jeered and rejoiced, mocked him through the iron bars his first night away from home: "Don't worry, stupid cat," he said, spitting alcohol in his eyes. "Gonna take real good care of you, yessir we are. Of course it is so... why would I lie to you?"

*

A man went in search of a tiger. He wanted to put the poor creature out of its misery. How alone it must feel in such a small place. He searched and searched, staggering in vain for hours until he found himself deep within the tangled bowels of a subway station. When he had followed the tracks far enough as to be away from all other people, he removed the knife from his coat and stood staring at a crack in the bricks on the wall, trying to steady his hand. The samurai had been precise; this had been of some importance, the man presumed, as otherwise there would be excruciating pain. The samurai had made it look easy. It seemed much more technical now, as the knife's edge trembled over the contours of his chest. There were angles to consider. The man wrapped both hands around the hilt, sighing five times. Long breaths that beckoned eternities. Then, he accidentally dropped the knife on the tracks below, which seemed like an abyss. There was a clang followed by a quick hiss, a tang in the air like metal burning. The man cursed under his breath then bent down, trying to recover his father's only heirloom. There was sweat trickling down his brow as he struggled to reach it. His hair started to blow with a mighty whoosh, bright boom of light flashing as the train screamed by. It took the knife with it. The man stood, marinating in his shame. Considered briefly leaping onto the track before deeming it too messy, which was just another excuse. He was a fuckup; all his life he had been a fuckup; why would the manner of his death be any different? He wanted to scream but nothing came out. He wanted to live but didn't know how. Behind him, a child was crying. Of course it is so... why would I lie to you?

*

A tiger went in search of a man. A tiny one would do just as well. He wanted to put the poor creature out of its misery. He had been tracking it for some time, following a trail of whiny tears and fearful bawling. The tiger felt a slick thrill down his spine being on the hunt again. This place resembled the one from his dreams where he would hunt often, the bricks were the same. It would be a mercy; the tiny human wouldn't last long. He, too, would be taken and domesticated. His wildness stolen from him. Coming down the stairs, the tiger narrowed his elliptical eyes. His tongue swished silently, swapping the juts of his teeth, a cleansing rinse. The child cried louder. Then there was another human, on the same side of the manmade chasm. Like all the other cowards though he immediately faced away, turning his back to the cat. But unlike the others, this one had no mask. His face was his mask and he was shuddering now, shaking with mortal fear. The tiger could smell it and it was delicious, mere appetizer to a greater, final feast to come. Childmeat tasted sweet like blood and berries, a wild tiger had once told him. Of course it is so... why would I lie to you?

*

A man went in search of a tiger. He wanted to live and to die, both. The tiger too, because he had never met a man worthy of slaughter before. All the warriors were gone; no lightning lived in their veins. Except the one facing him now, whose hands were steady, feet planted firmly. Mirrors in his eyes shone back a tiger's prodigious silhouette; an equal but opposite mirror flickered through the tiger's eyes making the man seem much taller, then there arose a flame of wrath beginning in the big cat's gut and vibrating out through his throat. Its fatal echo resounding through the station as the tiger lunged toward the man, who dared not move until the moment he did. There was no way for the cat to negate his own momentum by then, driven by rage red as blood and berry. Tumbling onto the tracks, the tiger fried. The man, who could not see the exquisite sparks, could feel their heat on the back of his neck. It was a noble death, bright as the first and last night on Earth. Of course it is so... why would I lie to you?

*

In another version of this story the tiger and man switch souls upon locking eyes. The child, so baffled by what he witnesses, has no choice but to become a writer in a futile attempt to explain the unexplainable. This version is a tragedy.

*

In yet another version, the man attempts seppuku but messes it up so badly that he ends up juggling his own entrails like a game of slippery hot potato. This version is a comedy.

*

A man went in search of a tiger.

A tiger went in search of a man.

They both found one.

Of course it is so... why would I lie to you?

Matthew Burnside

Centrifugal

# MESSAGES LEFT ON THE COSMIC ANSWERING MACHINE OF THE ANGELS CHARGED WITH RESPONDING TO LOST ORISONS (I.E. MISPLACED PRAYERS DEPARTMENT)

Dear Whoever,

Do you know what it feels like to miss someone you've never met?

What you took from me, I hate you for. You should know that. If we're going to talk like this, we need to be honest from the get-go. Fuck your halos, fuck your harps, fuck your wings & fuck your kingdom. Most of all, fuck your boss.

I'm sorry for my anger. It's just that grief is a tripwire & I am all ankles lately.

I'm trying. I really am, but it's hard to know falling in hate is just as easy as falling in love.

I don't want to hate you but it's you who made this hate possible & I cannot conceive of what you are anymore.

Anyway, I am all out of sorrow & so very full. I have wept more tears than there is sand. All out of salt now. Going dry. Send the gulls to take me away.

To you my darling: I love you like there's a hook in my heart & you are all the fish in the sea.

*

DEAR GOD-Y GOD GOD,

So hey. It's me!

Long time listener, first time caller. Big fan of the big guy.

Ma told me you I shouldn't worry about you not hearing this – you hear EVERYTHING, I've been assured - but I see how the internet messes up sometimes so I'm wearing these rabbit ears to amplify the signal just in case. I know I prob look dumb as shit right now but hopefully it does the trick?

Shit, also I'm sorry for saying shit! I try not to but it's a hard habit to kick and sometimes I don't even realize I'm saying it and my mom gets mad as shit about it but it's something I'm working on it.

So, I have like a real important question and at Sunday School the dude told me I should ask you: Dog Heaven IS in Human Heaven, right? Like, obviously it's a lil ways away and like maybe you have to take a cloud train to get there or whatever but it's connected, right? Like, technically. Like in Disney World where you have all the other parks within driving distance?

I only ask because a month ago our puppydog Gingersnaps got sick and crawled under the couch and never came out again and I had never thought about death before but I got to thinkin about it and it doesn't really scare me all that much– not trying to be a hardass or anything! LOL. But yeah, I did start thinkin about how if I'm in Human Heaven and can't see Gingersnaps or could only see her like once or twice an eternity or whatever – not sure how infinity works? – how much suckage that would be. So, like if it's possible whenever I do die, and I know it's something that's going to happen to everyone eventually and I'm not trying to change that, if you could just put me as close to Dog Heaven as possible that would be so excellent!

That's it for now, I guess? Also, if could shoot me another kid sister that would be rad.

Oh, one more thing: if Human Heaven was so perfect why was that Satan dude so sad and angry?

Really hope you're real and hearing this. Alright. Gonna take off these dumbass rabbit ears now.

Shit. Sorry.

*

To  Whom  It  May  Concern:

I  am  typing  this  so  you  cant  trace it,  then  will  burn  it.

Just  in  case  there  is  salvation,  I trust  this  confession  will  prove legally  binding  to  spare  damnation of  my  immortal  soul.

PS:  You  will  never  find  the  body.

*

Deer Toof Ferry,

Pleas keep yore monies and jist lemme keep my toof.  I repeet: Do not remove from under my pillo tonite pleas as it is my faverite toof, whose name is Charlie.

Thank you!!!

*

Dear Old Friend,

It's been many years since I stopped believing in miracles.

You know why.

I have listened well to hear your voice again only to find silence, swallowing all the words I once spoke with such conviction to my own congregation.

I was sure that I was right, but long years have scratched away the hate and it occurred to me one morning that maybe your voice speaks to us in other ways—the way ducks waddle along the edge of the lake with a bellyful of bread. The glowing eyes of my grandchildren bouncing on one knee and the laughter of rain.

Maybe you have been talking this whole time and we haven't been listening because maybe miracles hurt. Maybe their beauty is too much to bear—a beauty that's more like hunger, the way wolves howl out with wildness or poets pine for the moon.

I don't pretend to understand your ways. We are so very small. But I have to believe you haven't forsaken your love for all the small things.

I have to believe.

Sincerely,

Something Small

Centrifugal

# DIGITAL DREAMING IN ANALOG

## TUTORIAL

It was on the thirteenth stage of one of those marble simulator games that Maxwell encountered a glitch and accidentally stole a glimpse of eternity. He was rolling full tilt toward the prismatic net when a ghost sparrow distracted him and he shot off a little too far to the right, ending up on the wrong side of the level. Plunging through the hexagonal plane, he emerged spinning infinities on the other end, sparking blue sparks faster and faster until the console was whirring and the screen was flashing and the power went off in his parent's house. Speed runs were Maxwell's thing, which he would record fastidiously and upload to the internet. He liked that everything had to be impeccable, perfect. There was no room for failure in a speed run, and it was a rush; thrashmetal made the best soundtracks for these burst sessions. More than that, it enabled you to skip all the bad parts. Before he discovered this mode of play, he often found himself bored. Slow-churning death by tedium. Walking to the breaker in the basement, fumbling with a flashlight and nearly tripping over the completed Rubik's Cube on the 13th step, he suddenly felt dizzy and had to sit down. It was there he perceived something funny—a matrix of fractals whirling in the space behind his eyelids. In the darkness it seemed to be expanding now, wrapping around him, neon ribbons making a perfect sphere. He could see it still when he rose, crossing the abyss and flipping the breaker. Except this time when the lights came up he didn't recognize his surroundings. He could clearly make out the giant ball of light in which he was now encased, which he found he was unable to move forward in. A giant human hamster. The glowing shell of the sphere remained inflexible, pinned in place by something inexplicable.

## LEVEL ONE

Maxwell recognized the house as his own, except it wasn't his house now? It was his house from ten years ago. The shaggy orange carpet betrayed its dated interior décor. He recognized the Rubik's Cube on the steps of the pull-down ladder that ascended to the attic, which was incomplete now and brand new again: a fresh flurry of colors with no rhyme or reason, no order or distinction of pattern. Beautiful randomness. He watched himself (except it wasn't himself now, it was himself from ten years ago?) graze by his bubble, scoop up the cube, and pull himself into the attic. He could hear his parents yelling now, as they yelled so very often then, before the divorce. He watched himself = younger him = frantically flipping the dimensions of the cube at the edge of the attic, legs dangling down. He remembered: if he could just complete it, the bad times would pass. His hands raced faster now, the yelling growing louder, unkinder. Maxwell didn't mind the moment passing. He let it. The glowing shell of the sphere began to spin, slow-churning forward yet remaining in place, fixed in its axis by something inexplicable.

## LEVEL TWO

Then he was throwing up outside the school, his first day of elementary. This time his bubble was further from his younger self, rolling a little faster levitating a few feet off the earth, his view occasionally obscured by other students filing into the ugly salmon-colored brick building, which he hated the smell of; it would live inside his nostrils forever. Little Maxwell spat, picked up his backpack, shoved the Rubik's Cube back into the pocket, each side a little closer to uniformity, and entered the school. Maxwell didn't particularly mind the moment passing. The still-quite-bright-but-slightly-paler shell of the sphere spun on, trapped in a time loop by something inexplicable.

## LEVEL THREE

The next clip comes in a rush—concussive parade of consciousness, a broken carousel galloping too fast. Maxwell's first kiss on the trampoline with Portia Macintosh. Laughing with his brother, getting high beneath the highway underpass. The most uncomfortable birds and bees talk ever that turns out not so bad, the one beginning with dad knocking on the door, stuttering, blushing, preaching the virtues of abstinence before cutting the crap and saying, "Just be safe, kid, you've always been smarter than me...and when you love someone respect them because if you don't I promise you you'll lose them. All the good things will slip through your fingers and by the time you realize it it'll be too late." Maxwell's marble in the trees whirling faster now, spitting sparks. Obscured by a latticework of leaves. You could slow these ones down if you want, he mutters to no one in particular, watching his Rubik's Cube bouncing on a trampoline. Sides shifting into completion, nearly done. All meaningless. The sphere spins on, losing its luster, an inexplicable blur.

## LEVEL FOUR
LEVEL FOUR
LEVEL FOUR
LEVEL FOUR

Now comes everything that lies beyond, too far away to touch—weddings, babies, births, funerals. Maxwell's marble a dot in the sky. All love, all hate, every delicious semblance of in-between. Rubik's Cube an eye in the sun all colors sealed, fixed in their fates. Be kind rewind, Maxwell chants. His sphere an imperceptive gyre tumbling through eternities. Inexplicable.

**That's it! Maxwell thinks. Reaches his hand into the sun, plucks out a Rubik's Cube. Rewinds it. Twists all the colors backwards into a beautiful, senseless disarray.**

SECRET LEVEL?

Back home again, Maxwell blinked away a gauze of tears. He ran to hug his father and his mother in the living room and punched his brother playfully on the shoulder. He texted Portia, "You are all I ever think about. Don't slip through my fingers." Later that night, he turned on his system and played through at normal speed, without recording this time. He wondered whether the marble was moving or the world around the marble was moving; whether his life was moving or everything around his life was moving. Afterward, he peeled all the stickers off his Rubik's Cube and lay his head down on his pillow to dream.

The inexplicable future could be wonderful.

Centrifugal

# CAUSTICS: A LOVE STORY

Dearest Mother,

There are a couple ghosts fucking in my attic.

I don't know why the dead always choose my house to party but they do.

I've tried everything to rid my house of these ectoplasmic orgies: sweet saint-scented candles, astrologically enhanced crystals, discount demon chalk, even fancy gizmos like the Gordian Net & telekinetic tripwire from amateurghostkillers. com.

&&&

I once asked a professional why ghosts are always getting fresh in my attic & he remarked something about paraschematics. All those sharp angles & temporal folds. Sexy, sexy symmetry.

The dead don't dance through just any old house, he said: they hunt & hump & haunt where they hunt & hump & haunt for a reason, none of them petty. None of them to be trifled with.

But I don't buy that. They do it, I know, because they sense how lonely the living are. Can sniff it out on us & on me in particular.

Well, I'm tired of hearing their phantom shins sandpapering wood.

I'm tired of being subjected to the effortless joy of incorporeal ecstasy.

I'm tired of all these smug spirits rubbing their pleasure in my still-alive face.

So tonight, it ends: I'm going to fuck these ghosts.

&&&

I asked that same professional how one might go about seducing a ghost.

Why do you ask?

Just asking for a friend, I replied.

You have a friend?

&&&

After some Wikipedia research, I confirm my initial suspicions: peanut butter is, indeed, an aphrodisiac for amorous swinging ghosts.

&&&

Up to my elbows smothered in Jif® Whips®, I find myself reading poetry to the ghosts in my attic at midnight on a weekend. Surely that'll get 'em warmed up?

First I try ee cummings, but apparently that's just the guy's name & not the subject of his poetry. At least I don't think it is? It's hard to tell; nothing is capitalized.

Then I throw some Bukowski their way but that just makes them the opposite of horny, as it should. A sharp whistle of wind sends my book sailing through a lone & slanted witch window.

Finally, I read aloud some Poe.

*And travellers, now, within that valley, / Through the red-litten windows see...*

As I enunciate those syllables, splinters begin rising in wood. Nails are knotting themselves.

*Vast forms, that move fantastically / To a discordant melody...*

Lightbulbs are blinking, flashhappy filaments strobing like a miniboss moments before defeat.

*While, like a ghastly rapid river, / Through the pale door...*

Up through oaken boards leaps an electric shiver! Enough to curl my toes like crusty seahorses.

*A hideous throng rush out forever / And laugh- but smile no more.*

Soon my neck is a bentback spoon. There are ants in my pants; bees in my knees. My cuticles are bright neon milk, dripping quicksilver. Even my molars are vibrating, possessed with forbidden secret heat now. Little bombs of sawtooth tremor that feel the way peripheral drift looks... the way the phrase Penrose Staircase curls itself around a well-torqued tongue.

&&&

*Someone send the Trembulance!* I shout before passing out.

&&&

Dearest Mother,

It has been 3 months now since the incident.

For 3 months, I have been returning to this attic every night.

Honestly, I don't know how to make them leave.

I believe them to be as addicted to me as I am to them.

I'm not really sure what to do & I'm starting to run out of peanut butter.

Also, I really wish I hadn't told you any of this.

&&&

Dearest Mother,

Tonight I resolved to join the league of the living again.

One cannot fuck the dead forever, I suppose. You know—*that old chestnut.*

I have come up with a plan but I'm not sure about the logistics.

I'm not certain if it'll work. But one must try.

One must try to live while alive, right?

&&&

Dearest Mother,

I have done the deed & the deed wasn't easy.

My original plan involved a waffle maker, 33 golf tees, & a trident I stole from a theme park that rhymes with Fizney World. My original plan didn't pan out, it just made everything worse.

Long story.

But I'm happy to report I was finally able to untether myself from this rather tricky pleasure triangle.

In the end, I told them the truth.

Told them they had been wonderful, each night more blessed than the last. & I think they could sense this was the truth of it. Through the temporal ether, as they licked my tears clean, I could feel all my mortal fears shrinking. Could feel something that was real & beautiful folding itself gently into memory. It's not you *it's me*, I told them.

& at that moment, with everything in the house levitating save the lump in my throat & never-ending gratitude in my heart, a bittersweet breeze blew them out that crooked window into the lean, long night never to be heard from again.

&&&

It's like you always told me: *Don't put all your eggs in one basket.*

Now I finally understand, by eggs you meant love. And, by basket, of course, two horny ghosts.

I love you mom.

Happy Mother's Day.

Centrifugal

# INFINITY PARADISE OBLIVION CUBICLE

When you've finally had enough go to the designated vending machine, the one on the corner of Sidereal & Main, take out the little slip of paper—the one you pocketed from that strangely glowing misfortune cookie with the unique alphanumeric sixty-five-string-long-combination. Carefully punch in the numbers, letters, symbols. When it opens, squeeze yourself inside, close the door behind you, and upon hearing it latch shut forever with a pneumatic hiss, never go back to that dreaded place from whence you came. Life inside the vending machine will at the outset seem very crammed. Your back may have to adjust some, spine curving to acclimate to the crookedness of the interior, curlicue teeth of springs poking at your knees, hips, bellybutton. You may suspect you made a terrible mistake, but in time you'll find it's bigger on the inside. And it will be dark, very dark at first, until someone comes along to type in 'lightbulb' at which point a lightbulb will appear over your head, granting you just enough grace to behold your own digits again. This is a reverse vending machine, you see, and people are more generous than you think—their donations will be gracious. Then one day some kind soul will type in 'book' and 'reading glasses' and, though it will still be a very tight fit you will at least have something to clutch between your digits then, and even more, something to clutch in your mind. It will be enough, just enough, to distract from the lack of wiggle room. At this point most passersby will still grimace as they pass you on the street: *What a life! Can you imagine being stuck in a tiny cubicle for eternity? Can you fathom what kind of person would voluntarily choose such a life?* they'll remark to their bewildered companions, as you ogle back face squished against the cold glass. It may be small in here but that doesn't make the world out there any less smaller, you'll think, returning to your book. You know what you're about. One day someone will snap a Twitpic of you and you'll go viral. Perhaps it's just pity but from that point on the more extravagant donations will flood in. Like I said, it's bigger on the inside. This reverse vending machine expands. Is elastic—like all magic boxes. The litany of gifts will come in a stream, a rush of generosity: "Blanket" + "Good Tasting Food" + "Toilet" + "Toilet Paper" + "Wine" + "Comfortable Chair" + "Incense" + "Furry Slippers" + "Fancy Robe" + "Smoking Pipe" + "Newspaper" + "Record Player" + "Voluminous Collection of Records" + Etc. The passersby who previously grimaced at you will grimace no longer, instead growing slightly pink with envy: *Why do they get all that free stuff? Why do they deserve it? Why not me?* One day, a wealthy donor types in "Beach" and this, perhaps, is where the real trouble begins, when the trolls show up. "You can't have a beach without a shark!" laughs one kid mischievously while typing in "Great White"... later, he and his friends nearly pass out watching its fin tracing its way toward you through the waves. The look on your face, flush and fear-stricken, paddling for dear life back to the sand. All the bad things come out of the woodworks, then: "Tornado" + "Bear" + "Centipedes" + "Booby Traps" + "Quicksand" + "Candy Corns". Crowds gather to watch you struggle, escape the next novel scenario by the skin of your teeth. It's televised, in fact, highest rated show in history, pre-approved for ten seasons. The donations turn wickedly imaginative, insidiously effective, determined by dial-in fan voting: "Carpet Made of Legos" + "Barbwire Bed" + "Bomb in a Birthday Cake" + "Rain of Needles". In the season finale, finally another person is added into the mix but fated to end badly when the host types in "Heartbreak" which proves all the rage for ratings... all the punishment you've endured is nothing next to losing them instead. You want to weep but can't, nothing comes out, because no one has donated "Tears". Banging on the glass, you beg: *Just me, please. Drag me through the abyss. Concoct a new hell every hour. But make it mine and nobody else's.* Well this is no fun, watchers will say then. This show has really jumped the shark! All donations will cease. No one will walk by your vending machine anymore and, in time, it will shrink back down to its original size. You will be grateful to feel the little springs jabbing into your sides again, your measly book that you've read a hundred times. Your one dim and lonely lightbulb. One day someone unplugs the machine. Silence is nice, darkness too, but only ever for a little while. One day vandals shatter the glass with a sledgehammer, and you step back out into the world, never to return to that dreaded place from whence you came. Life outside the vending machine will seem very scary at first, very scary indeed. You may suspect you made a terrible mistake, but in time you'll find it's bigger on the outside.

Centrifugal

# PAN'S LOBOTOMY

None of us can find the door if there even is one. I'm not so sure anymore. We have been searching for two billion years now, give or take a golden era. Licking the walls of the apartment, groping the darkness for doorknobs the way blind men feel for Braille, flopping around on the carpet like epileptic sardines in a Technicolor tin. We = four of us: Logos, Psyche, Dynamis, and me, Aporia. Maybe more. Sofa makes five.

The first day we crushed up the stuff and put it in every orifice. We felt colors and saw textures. I had a conversation with the number '6'. Logos floated balloons out the window bearing little messages, gems like HAPPINESS IS A WARM GERM or MOTHERFUCK THE ONE WITH THE GOLDEN GUN. Psyche in the acid jacket made a necklace out of baby teeth while Dynamis burned the bed sheets in the washing machine, mixed the ashes with rubber cement and smothered it on 'Cat', which is the name of his dog. I devoured random selections from infinity's jukebox.

With night came a ramshackle parade in the sky of inflated Buddhas and plastic Jesuses. We feasted on shish kebobs of human tissue and calcified phlegm, clew and coagulated mercury, washed it down with vials of bone marrow, pearls we plucked from our tear ducts with tweezers. Treated ourselves to dessert of knife soup and caramelized melancholy.

"Off to the store for Zero Dream Apparatus," Logos told us, and Psyche warned him: "Nay. Into the exploding fog." He sat back down. Fed Cat to Sofa. "Ennui." Eternal consciousness was his curse.

Sofa bellowed, gnashed its cushions. That's when we saw the symbol emblazoned on the floor, bright as a seraph.

#

"Is?" Logos said. We concurred.

Someone had left their baby harnessed to the end of a pendulum dangling from a serpent's tail. The violet dagger-shaped eyes of the baby cascaded a viscous fluid, which crept between my toes and puddled its way up my thighs until it found my belly button, sucked itself through the hole. "I am entered," I averred. Logos opened his mouth wide, projected a monolith on the wall. "Behold: The shimmering architecture of the soul's lattice." Dynamis set fire to the baby, captured the effervescent blue smoke in a bottle and buried it in his ribcage.

"Is?" Logos repeated.

"Apotheosis-bound," Psyche said, and proceeded to do calculations on a razorblade pillow. It thrashed and howled, but we held it down while she did the math, blazing the luminiferous chalk against its contours until it became domesticated, its barbs wailing and wilting off.

$$\infty \times \infty / \infty\infty (\infty + \infty) + \infty 2 - \infty = ?$$

"To kingdom come!" She deciphered, but we didn't follow. Eternal logic was her curse. "Salamanders?" Logos asked, and she traced the equation once more. "Gallop thy atoms westward, against the grain," she explained. We nodded. There were winged cogs in the air and Logos plucked one. Unzipped his skull and put it away for safe keeping.

The immeasurable evening was then spent in exaltation of our sublime ignorance. We consecrated the formlessness of our egos and the splendor of our toenails, worshipped the almighty circle while brandishing ketchup packets. We embodied mountains and oceans and constellations and insects and empires and gods and devils with our vile mimicry. Then we disconnected our bodies, unsnapped the puzzle pieces of our organs and traded. Dressed ourselves in each other's fashionable flesh and copulated with mirrors. We reveled in ecstasy until the drugs began to wear off, and Logos stabbed the nothingness with a murderous zeal. "Art thou Art." Psyche corrected him. "Thou art Thou."

Sobered now, we collect ourselves. Scoop the slumber out of our third eyes. Sunlight is guttering in through the apartment windows; we bask in its warm, irrefutable truth. "We should find the door before it's too late," Psyche reasons, as Dynamis grips a sledgehammer. He swings into a window full force—yawping like a savage—but the pane bends reflexively to evade the blunt edge. "Not like that," Psyche says. "It's a simulacrum, remember? Facade." Logos has already begun peeling up the carpet.

I stand in the corner, yawning while the others slaver for the exit. Congealed memory drizzles down my neck from a hole in my head. I stuff a cork in the wound. The others do not accept me as one of them now. They ignore me in this state. I am a mere phantom automaton.

"Or maybe the answer is here," Psyche suggests, rubbing the marking on the floor with a scientist's scrutiny.

#

"Maybe it has everything to do with everything," she says.

"What does it mean?" asks Logos. Dynamis thrusts and flails his sledgehammer in the background, just to give his hands something to do. He lusts for destruction of matter, but there is nothing left to pulverize in the room. He begins to unclasp his mandible. "No, Dynamis," Psyche says. "Hold together." Ruefully, he clicks his jaw back on. Eternal boredom is his curse. If Psyche were not here, he would happily tear himself apart and eat his own tart bones. Savor the succulent sinews and corpuscles.

Logos rips the last shred of carpet up. Nothing.

Psyche turns toward me now, heaps suspicion upon me as gravediggers heap dirt upon the dead. "YOU—you know where the exit is, don't you?" Suddenly I am one of the tribe again. I nod meekly, reach up and unplug the cork from my wound. Allow the memory to flow freely, spitting like a fountain. One-by-one, my brothers and sister lap it with their tongues until they thirst no longer. I imbibe it, too, for I am weak. This room is the only home I have ever known: the only reality I trust. Eternal doubt is my curse.

In no time the room has repaired itself. The carpet has grown back thicker—a stubborn exoskeleton for restless nomads of the mind. That baby is back, too, taunting us from the ceiling with two pensive, hollow sockets.

There is a bowl on the coffee table filled to the brim with white corpulent fruit. A note invites us to gorge ourselves.

Logos notices a mysterious marking underfoot.

#

"Is?" he wonders. Nobody knows.

That night, we crush up the fruit and put it in every orifice. Feel colors and see textures. I have a conversation with the number '7'. Logos floats balloons out the window bearing little messages, gems like HAPPINESS IS A LUKEWARM GERM or MOTHERFUCK THE ONE WITH THE SILVER GUN. Psyche in the acid jacket makes earrings out of baby teeth while Dynamis burns the bed sheets in the washing machine, mixes the ashes with rubber cement and smothers it on 'Fish', which is the name of his lizard. I devour random selections from infinity's jukebox.

None of us can find the door, if there even is one. I'm not so sure anymore. We have been searching for two and a half billion years now, give or take a golden era.

Centrifugal

# PROCESSION OF THE DOGFACE LEPERS

"The one thing nobody can do for you is walk on your own two feet."

—Old Dogface proverb

*...12...13...14...15...16...17...18...19...20...21...22...23...24...*

(Once a year, we clear the streets for the dogface lepers. Old as sea, sun, and star, the Festival of Maw has been the most prized of my people's traditions since the beginning of our recorded history. The horned hail from all directions: north, south, east and west. In ragged droves and clanking caravans they come, snaking through hills and treading sharp-pebbled beaches, marching the sun-baked cobble streets of Lamsdown, weighty cowbells swinging from the necks of the adults and tinsel chimes tinkling on the children's dainty wrists. Barefoot and threadbare they walk—day and night, without rest, without drink—suffering the elements and bearing their burden in silence and humility. Some will sew their mouths shut in protest while others haul impossibly cumbersome items strapped on their backs in lieu of the conventional albatrosses. Lead anvils; sacks of dirt, sand, or seed; grandfather clocks; bedposts; small, uprooted trees; rubber tires; anything to spite the cruel lot of my tribe who go out of their way to make the long pilgrimage even more oppressive than it already is. Those who relish the migration of the lepers like sport plant thorns or spread broken glass ahead of time along the *Trails of the Filthy*, pelt the Dogfaces with soured trash or spoiled food as they pass by their village. They'll enjoy chilled purified water in their presence, a delicacy afforded only to those born of my caste, while the Dogfaces grow up drinking from the streams where we deposit our refuse, in which we urinate and defecate and dispose of our dead and contaminated. All along the trails around festival time, you'll spy horned dolls strung from tree limbs, snouts stitched smiling to mock the horned ones. At festival's end, each doll is clipped down and tossed into the stream. Righteous children like me wave to them floating out to sea while adults rejoice for the purification of the kingdom for another year. If perchance it rains during the festival, Dogface mothers might be seen lashing their young with a look, curt reminders to accept not one drop on their tongues, for it is taboo, a weakness and therefore against their way. At times, a Dogface child will pass out from exhaustion, the mother or father will scoop, hoist them up, carry them for many miles. If they wake before reaching the destination, they are immediately placed back on their own two feet to finish the trek alone. *Almost there, my beautiful child*, I once heard a Dogface dare to whisper to her son, a child with abnormally protrudent horns for his age. *No crying, do not allow them that.* A stark sunless face tried its best to bury tears of shame, but I saw them clinging to his chin before being absorbed by his mother's skirt. The boy saw that I saw, too. I could not look him in the eye. When they made it to the edge of the cliff—what is known as The Maw to us but to them, simply: The Long Bridge Home—that same boy waved at me, then dove knees first into the icy waters below. Steam rose slow, there was a howl deep beneath the waves, a red cloud which crept up to the surface, spreading like a blanket unfurling upon the sea's livid skin. Blossoming out, swirling like rose-colored wine. One by one they pitched themselves off the precipice after that, paying the price of our sins so we wouldn't have to. I wonder sometimes why I wasn't born a Dogface. Why I was born clean, without a scar on my soul. Why me? Why not them? Why not that boy? Mother scolds me for entertaining these thoughts. *You are what you are. They are what they are. He that made Us made Them. All is right as rain*, she tries to put me at ease, but her logic only confuses me, angers me more. Father forbids wrestling with such nonsense. Reminds me *What if?* is a dangerous thought, maybe the most dangerous of all thoughts. Still. I can't help it. Secretly, I admire them. To swallow slaughter with such grace is an art. The Dogfaces are artists. They are beautiful to me. We bleed the same blood: blood without a face. Weep the same salt of sadness. I don't believe in the old way, but who am I to challenge the elders? To defy sea, sun, and star? Tonight is the night before the festival and I lie awake haunted by a hand that won't stop waving to me and only me; a phantom splash that won't stop hammering home the silence in my head. No matter what I do, I keep seeing those bodies float up to the surface. Too many to count, innumerable as the stars and their infinite wisdom. Yet I try and count them all, give each driftwood corpse a name. This is the punishment I give myself. I won't sleep until I have counted them all. I can't ever count them all. But all is right as rain, I am told. Something is wrong with the rain.)

*...1011...1012...1013...1014...1015...*

# THE ARTIST OF THE UGLY

"Creation is hard"

—God

## _The Incident_

The pensive screen blinked and The Writer could feel his heart pinging. Thirteen years of work, one page, swallowed into an abyss of lost-forever sentences in less than a second. Manically he stroked his chin, as if his beard were dripping off. Waves of grief passed over him. Perhaps not wholly irrecoverable? The single-sentence, semicolon-clad monolith of a manuscript tentatively titled Into the Breathless Mouth of Babylon by M. Burnside, was to be the second piece in his sophomore collection. Was to be, when there came that wrenching crunch, ungodly cough of circuitry within the plasticine peach-thin skin of laptop, not unlike a spork dropped into a blender, as he was forced to witness the sight of so marvelously wrought a thing - a string of script so carefully crystallized in an amber of text, sculpted from sap of time insoluble – vanish: _Vamoose c'est la vie voila!_ - and, in so doing, solidify his obscurity for time immemorial.

## _The Circumstances Of The Muse's Communion_

You could have a steam train—Peter Gabriel had been singing, just before the incident—if you just lay down your tracks. Taunting The Writer through the speaker of an old, battered radio buried under three floors of oaken board in the basement, as if underwater, one golden oldie after another slid in among the meandering stations between Bjork's *It's Oh So Quiet* & Fleetwood Mac's *Landslide*. Mister Giddy, his lackadaisical calico, had been watching him work, tail twitching along with the arrhythmic wind swarms thumping at the window frame, insistent to intrude into his master's quietude. At the moment of the consummate sentence's conception the cat had leapt, startled at the sound of a car crashing some blocks away. Just before that, The Writer had been thinking of submarines—their little periscopes peeking up out of the water. He could smell the sweet lemon-bitter scent of his tea whistling downstairs on the stove, ready to be imbibed, ready to birth so many galaxies like Proust's own demitasse.

## The Devil In The Details

A stroke of brilliance: If he could just recreate the conditions in which the muse had initially communed with him, maybe he could rewrite it exactly as it was, recapture the original in all its splendor & literary virtuosity?

## The Replication Of Genius

The initiative to replicate his original genius began without a hitch, at first. Buying a replacement laptop and opening a new document was easy enough, but complications arose almost immediately upon hiring the driver to crash their car around the block. The screeching of the wheels was off, and it was an expensive ordeal. It occurred to The Writer that perhaps no one crash could be duplicated. Still, he knew he must try. Again! He texted the driver, inspiration swirling in the space of his irises. The songs came next. It wasn't enough to request just the one song, he had to hear all three songs in a row, in the right order no less. This involved quite some waiting on the line to the radio station,  then a great deal of explanation standing in the kitchen scribbling spirals on a newspaper. Filling a bathtub with toy submarines proved relatively less complicated, though tedious, as some of the plastic vessels were prone to flipping upside-down in the water. Getting the buoyancy levels right by filling them with just the right amount of water was tricky. All things considered, remaking tea was the easiest of the tasks, then waiting for it to boil.

## *The Wrench In The Plans*

But then there was the matter of the cats: the circus of cats in harnesses dangling like a feline trapeze troupe, ballet of paws none touching the floor, mewling as they bobbled up and down, tails writhing undulating with indifference. Mister Giddy had proven stubborn, unwilling to partake in The Writer's collaboration. The choreography was wrong, the angle at which he jumped when the car went skidding tragically inaccurate, not to mention each time it crashed it became somewhat less startling to the cat, who came to expect it, finding it more and more unsurprising. This is how The Writer came to gather up all the cats in the neighborhood, rigging up the contraption of an elaborate mobile—a series of swings custom-built so each could be suspended in mid-air all at once. Surely one of them would get the angle right, lunging the way it was supposed to? This assumption proved erroneous, as all the cats interconnected at once resulted in each cat sensing the movements of the other, bouncing off cue. Again! He commanded the cats, inspiration swirling in the space of his irises. *You could have a steam train*—Peter Gabriel sang, taunting The Writer—*if you just lay down your tracks.* When the right words finally came they came in a dizzying rush, a lapse of wizardry, words flowing direct from the fingers of the muse into his own, as the car crashed perfectly and the cats danced and the periscopes peeked. He could smell the sweet lemon-bitter scent of his tea whistling downstairs on the stove, along with something else now too? Paper burning… all those spirals consumed.

## THE MASTERPIECE

And anyone whose head happened to be curling around a curtain to steal a peek at the scene that afternoon might see the firetruck sprawled in the cul-de-sac flashing its silent alarm. Might see The Writer standing in his driveway, cavalcade of cats at his back, one perched on his shoulder blade yawning nonchalantly. Might see the man's head tipping back, howling with laughter at the spectacle of it all. Inscrutable, maddening spectacle of it all. He's lost it, they might conclude. They might be right.

"Your house, sir" they might overhear one of the fire fighters murmur to the man.

"What?"

"Your house, sir. It's burning down."

"Yes. Thank you, my good man. Yes—So it is. I can see that now."

Matthew Burnside

Centrifugal

# AN ADVENT CALENDAR TO ASSAY THE STILL-BEATING OF THE DOLOROUSLY HEARTSICK

*to be used sparingly, in the 25 days immediately following a broken heart; if symptoms persist, consult your physician or psychic

DAY ONE: A single bee will emerge to sting your nose. Can you feel it? Does it hurt? That means you're still alive.

DAY TWO: A swatch of their scent. In time there will be other smells, equally beautiful. If you can imagine other perfumes, that means you're still alive.

DAY THREE: A lock of their hair and a match. If you accidentally burn your finger, that's good. That means you're still alive.

DAY FOUR: A love letter and pair of baby scissors. Make some confetti. In time there will be other things to celebrate, an occasion to use it. That means you're still alive.

DAY FIVE: A photograph and sharpie. Embellish their face with cartoonish flourishes—a mustache, devil horns, artistically subpar tattoos, etc. When you laugh, that means you're still alive.

DAY SIX: A shot. When it burns your throat going down, that means you're still alive.

DAY SEVEN: An iPod with your song. Listen to it until you realize how silly the lyrics are, how mediocre its melodic arrangements. When it sounds like noise instead of music, that means you're still alive.

DAY EIGHT: A twenty-dollar bill. Use it to buy yourself a meal, preferably something you want that they hated. Eat it alone, for the practice. In time food will taste flavorful again. That means you're still alive.

DAY NINE: A skeleton key. Use it to fill the space where their apartment key used to be. In time there will be other doors, other buildings, other rooms. When you can imagine moving through them, that means you're still alive.

DAY TEN: A sprig of mugwort. Eat it whenever you miss the malady of their kiss. In time there will be other lips, not as bitter. When you can taste them, that means you're still alive.

DAY ELEVEN: A pocket watch. Wind it. It's yours. The whole of a life isn't contingent on yesterdays. If you can hear the ticking, that means you're still alive.

DAY TWELVE: A mystery seed. Plant it. You'll have to wait around to see what it could be. When you can imagine other things growing, that means you're still alive.

DAY THIRTEEN: A fingernail? It's gross, I agree. As it withers, eventually decomposing, growing soft and sludge-like, seek something new. Anything beautiful can become ugly. When you can fathom the inverse again, that means you're still alive.

DAY FOURTEEN: A condom. When you can grasp its utility, that means you're still alive.

DAY FIFTEEN: A vial of ink. When you can imagine writing another name, that means you're still alive.

DAY SIXTEEN: A bookmark. Upon returning their books or getting all your books back that you let them borrow, use it to read something new. When you can relish words that don't just come out of a certain mouth, that means you're still alive.

DAY SEVENTEEN: A feather. Use it to trace a shape on your pillow that's not their face. When it's unmarred by any profile's impression but your own, that means you're still alive.

DAY EIGHTEEN: A round stone to skip across the lake. Nothing skips forever. When it sinks, that means you're still alive.

DAY NINETEEN: A fishhook, for all the other fish in the sea. When you can envision your boat adrift once more, that means you're still alive.

DAY TWENTY: A Russian doll. Take them apart. Throw one away. Put them back together. When the doll is fine, even with one part missing, that means you're still alive.

DAY TWENTY-ONE: A pair of dice. When you can see rolling them again, that means you're still alive.

DAY TWENTY-TWO: A placebo pill. When you realize it isn't necessary for your system to survive, that means you're still alive.

DAY TWENTY-THREE: A Lego brick. To step on every time you remember something they said that turned out to be untruthful in the end. When you can walk still, that means you're still alive.

DAY TWENTY-FOUR: A tiny snow globe. Shake it well, observe the flurries swirling. Accept the storm and its imminent passing. When there is serenity again, you will be able to see through the glass. In time there will be much else to see. That means you're still alive.

DAY TWENTY-FIVE: Another bee, but this one won't sting. Won't waste its sting on someone who wouldn't appreciate it. Its lancet will remain intact. It will move through the window, through the air, until it finds a field of flowers, lumbering toward its sweetness. In time it will inherit nectars, gather gardens. It will float on, biding its sweetness for a death worth dying for, which means it's still alive.

Matthew Burnside

Centrifugal

# RAMSHACKLE HEAVENS

In Ramshackle Heaven we lay our heads down to sleep on little pillows of paradise. Under patchwork stars, having traded butterflies for bricks, screaming for singing, cuts for kisses. We push our bodies together as close as we can stand it, bones bent, hands held prayerfully to keep our new home from crashing down atop our heads. Everyone huddled beneath the same hallowed, sagging ceiling... In Ramshackle Heaven everyone is invited and no one ever wants to go home because home is here, is you, is me, is us... In Ramshackle Heaven we honor the smallest bodies, the ones the world was quick to crush under its too-busy boots... In Ramshackle Heaven, we left the world outside when a child decided one day to build his pillow tent in the middle of the city. An exodus of exiles ready to begin again... In Ramshackle Heaven, there is no currency because there is nothing to buy that can't be bought with simple kindness and a scintilla of grace... In Ramshackle Heaven everyone sighs when the moon is visible through a cut in the cloth like a neon hangnail because it reminds us of the slenderest of wrists and it is, all of it, almost too much to bear but bear it we must... In Ramshackle Heaven it only ever rains when those of us in grief are weeping, but we have umbrellas made of each other now and interlocked pinkies to help us hide the hurt... In Ramshackle Heaven there are chandeliers in the shape of all the lights we lost along the way, whose flickering shadows slowdance along the wall the way hummingbirds gather pendulous petals for nesting—gentle as wingbeat yet soft as summer's laughter... In Ramshackle

Heaven, even the clichést of clichés can still be beautiful because the cynics are all outside… In Ramshackle Heaven, the north tent is reserved for the peace-eyed dreamers, the east tent for the couples who make love at midnight, the south tent for stray dogs and driftless cats, but the west tent is always left empty for the ghosts to speak their names aloud on the air stolen from them. In Ramshackle Heaven we still our tongues to clutch answers laced in the secret language of rain yet we remain dry forever. We do not forget the dead still living alive through us, by whose hearts such heavens are built. Shhhhhhhhhhhhhhhhhhhhhhh.

Listen close and you'll hear them too:

Matthew Burnside

Centrifugal

# DEAR WOLFMOTHER: A SERIAL NOVELLA

(AKA Atomic Girls Don't Cry,
AKA Malice in Wonderland,
AKA Petals Break Fast, Thorns Bleed the Breakers)

---

"Ladies and gentlemen, boys and girls, dying time's here"
-Dr. Dealgood, *Mad Max Beyond Thunderdome*

---

"The end of the world occurred pretty much as we had predicted.
Too many humans, not enough space or resources to go around.
The details are trivial and pointless.
The reasons, as always, purely human ones."
-Fallout 2

---

"Plaudite, amici, comedia finita est"
-Last Words of Beethoven (Allegedly)

Centrifugal

# ALLEGRO /// SUMMER

==========={BEGIN TRANSMISSION SEQUENCE}

=============<beaming live from Merrymouseland>

=============<AKA the merriest little place on earth>

: : : : : : : : : :

>> call me Coda—spirit daughter of the Motherwolf <<

>> whoevermaybehearingthis, anyone left out there in the blazing Scorch. Big Empty <<

>> listen well & listen fast: hurry to live in spite of the world! <<

>> watch the sky breathing glass, quicksilver to the touch <<

>> daybirds melting into its open mouth, caught on the fangs of too-sharp stars... <<

: : : : : : : : : :

==========={END TRANSMISSION SEQUENCE}

Come night, I'll count my bullets in peace. Seven tall: porcelain-painted, pretty as crackledile teeth.

Line 'em up and load 'em in.

No intruders shall enter, so long as there is blood left in these veins.

Build your walls high and gates unbreakable.

Overwhelm => Attack => Shatter

REPEAT: No outsiders permitted here.

*You've been warned.*

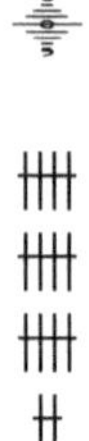

Seventeen months.

Seventeen and counting...

Holed up here, another night squished slantwise in a pirate's right socket.

Another night spent swallowing this wash-grey, garbled light. Counting slats crushing in between the cracks. Remember: if you can see them they can see you back. So much as light a candle they'd know it from miles away.

Teach yourself how to be at home in the shadows. Wear dark clothes as to easily melt – lapse into the jetty black like butter - and resist relying even on the faintest of moonglow.

Harbor a healthy hatred toward all that is light, which cannot be trusted.

Next, learn to pick out roving shapes in the darkness. Grainy oblongs, bouncing flits and flutters. Get good (better still) at squinting — practice makes perfect in this regard — and whatever you do never, ever shut your eyes for longer than it takes to reach the tippy top of Stormer's Cove*.

*21-minutes 50-seconds on quickfeet with the way I've rigged it, blocking the main stairs and draping the exterior path with a nexus of makeshift snares and tripwires stretched taut, fashioned from fancy ropes that once cordoned off bladder-bursting queues.

Just buying time, the lot of us.  No skin left to hide in. Borrowed bones with dust for blood...

Counting the ticky-tocks as they pass now. Rolling them around in my skull like those dice made of teeth some of the scabbers carry through the Scorch. Drowning all thought in the frothy broth of being. Big fuzzy nothing stew.

*Holy numbness; hollowed by thy name.        Amen.*

There is only one way left: Assassinate the future...assassinate the past...then assassinate every possibility of a self. Accept only the here and now forever.

A gnarly mask helps.          Wear your facelessness like a crown.

Finally, having trained your broken body to take burst-naps, remind yourself you'll never have a pleasant dream again.

Make no mistake, tourist: Every story is a/an ___________ story.

A)  apocalypse

B)  mystery

C)  horror

D)  revenge

*Shhhhhhhhh.*

Do you hear that?

Nothing.

Nevermind.

False alarm.

You wouldn't believe me, sitting where I'm sitting now seeing what I see from the top of

Stormer's Cove — Merrymouseland's second most popular attraction adapted from an antiquated cartoon featuring a rum-drunken pirate with conspicuously human cargo and a monochromatic, chattering Toucan named Rococo -- but it's all true: Once upon a time this sprawling, tetanus-filled wonderland was paradise. *Welcome to the merriest little place on Earth!*™ greeters would sing with forced grins at the gates, to which happy plastic families flocked dropping half a year's salary to soak up the state-of-the-art attractions. For adults, it was a place to voila the world simple again—as though it ever was. For kids, it was a place to be themselves, back when that was still legal, before the War of Seven Lambs took that from us, and so much more, too.

*Welcome to the Merriest Little Place on Earth!*

\- Said the last greeter left.
(Forced grin.)

Some splinters are best left unplucked from the mind, I guess.

For example, see that rust-hooked harpoon there? It's been hung on the wall of Stormer's Cove ever since the park's inaugural opening back in '26. At any time I could peel it off the wall and find out whether or not the ancient thing actually works or is actually just a glorified prop.

But I don't.

Don't ask me why.

Dear Wolfmother,

Thank you verily for the warmth of your fur. Come winter, may it keep me from catching cold.

I caught myself again today thinking of your great sacrifice. How I came upon you maimed in Kiddy Corner, bentback spattered-red hindleg and the other clamped tightly in the horrendous jaws of that albino beast. Cracklediles rarely ever venture so deep into the park, so it came as a surprise to find you both having it out smackdab in the midway. I half expected you were both animatronic, escapees from the Hall of Obscure Dignitaries. (I wouldn't have blamed you, by the way.)

But even then I confess the sight of you was majestic. Mane fluffed up, tail sharply at attention with your muscular mottled chest puffed out. Eyes electric—two blistering blue bolts and teeth bared. You were imperious with rage.

I knew then you were my mother. Not my human mother, of course, but the one I might have chosen for myself in a better world. Because even as you thrashed and fought for dear life, all snarl and claw, stabbing your teeth into the leathery back of that brute, I could see that you were positioning your frame in front of the downed concession shack, behind which your babies were whining and falling over each other in a panic. And even when I could see the blinding-white brute whipping around to catch your neck fatally in its great jutted mouth, hearing the bones beginning to crunch, you howled out not for yourself but for your children. I squeezed off a shot to end your suffering then, proceeding to finish off the bastard myself with my old railsword.

Just so you know: you were a good mother.

Bigger things should tend after those that are smaller.

This is not how the world works. Just how it should work.

Mercy here will only get you killed.

Still, know I am keeping an eye out for and on your babies. While they remain much too skittish to come to me when I offer them a Merrymaus Bar, they are free to roam within my domain untouched. I make sure to leave plenty of confections scattered around the park to feed the pack of four. I have also taken precautions at the West Gate now to keep out any rogue cracklediles.

I wouldn't worry too much. There's only one apex predator here and that's me.

I'll keep you informed. In the meantime, may you sleep in peace.

-C

<u>To-Do</u>
~~fortify west gate~~

~~fortify east gate~~<br>
~~transfer backup food cache from A3 to E5~~<br>
check perimeter bear traps and deadfalls<br>
mind the wolfpups<br>
procure stronger line for monorail nest pulley/test<br>
resew snatches of Mausenstein<br>
keep an eye out for scabbers, always<br>
stay the HELL away from any grimers<br>
stay vigilant<br>
live<br>
live<br>
live

One of Merrymouse's earliest cartoons featured a bumbling alien with buck teeth called Oofus the Space Cadet. Poor Oofus, left behind by his own kind. After exploring a faraway moon, a classic saucer UFO lifted up and away from the screen and nobody aboard noticed that Oofus was even missing. Nobody ever loved Oofus enough to notice. The whole cartoon was basically just that premise there: Oofus, alone, exploring a strange moon all on his lonesome getting swept into one misadventure after another.

In one episode, Oofus sculpts a little fort out of hardened moonsand and decides to guard it. (Who knows what he's guarding it from? This foreign cartoon moon was not like the Scorch, where there are real fiends to rob you, splay you out, make you suffer for sport. Or in the case of grimers, carve you up for prime organ real estate.) Maybe it was just something to do. Anyway, this endeavor gives Oofus a great deal of purpose, at least for an episode, and he even begins sculpting some fellow lookouts to keep him company and take over his shift whenever he gets tired. He begins talking to one of his moonsand friends, sort of narrating aloud everything he's doing and thinking. This particular moonsand friend has two polished geodes for eyes. They gleam when facing skyward, at one of two suns blazing off in the background like some Star Wars bullshit. This particular moonsand friend is his best friend in the whole wide galaxy. There's a little montage of him chatting up his moonsand mate: holding an umbrella over their heads to protect him from a meteor shower in one scene. Serving him some sculpted food on a flimsy plastic plate in another (a sandwich—what else?) In the last heartbreaking shot, one of those giant suns that's always looming in the backdrop zooms closer for some reason, melting his moonsand mate when Oofus has his back turned. Oofus struggles to rebuild his friend but the sun, deciding to remain where it's at now, tattooed into the foreground, won't allow it. Moonsand mate keeps melting, again and again, just as fast as Oofus can built him back up again. Oofus cries big fat tears that form a puddle in a crater on the moon, which Oofus eventually sits beside crying some more until he falls in and nearly drowns. Poor Oofus eventually paddles out and he is all alone again. Though he is alone, he continues to talk as if his friend is still there, narrating every last dumb detail.

There's power in this.

Oofus knew.

You're only alone if your mind accepts that you're alone.

The UFO never comes back for Oofus. And though he has every right to be angry, he's not. He's simply...lonely. Somehow, he finds a reason to laugh at least once every episode. To me, this makes him brave.

Six years ago was he last time I laughed at anything. I was six. Coincidentally, this was right before the government decided it was their sovereign right to claim all children as property of the state. Before all the adults agreed this wasn't outright insanity and the War of Seven Lambs began . . .

All cartoons are tragedies by default. Have you ever noticed that?

Anvils and dynamite, trick pistols and phantom floors that disappear the moment you look down. Prey flashing signs of irony as the predator fails to catch his life's desire, doomed by a sham corporation whose products never fail to arrive faulty.

We laugh at these poor characters because some artist somewhere has sketched them into obscurity, misfortune, and calamity. We are only able to laugh at their misery because it's not our own.

I'm not sure if I'm describing the definition of comedy or human nature here.

Beneath the park in the haunted tunnels there is an old transistor radio reserved for emergencies. It was there, when I first arrived, that I first transmitted my futile SOS for any strays left listening.

Sang my beacon out into a ravaged world.

>>> *It's over. The rich won. The callous, power-hungry and stone-hearted...* <<<

This world isn't made for dolls. I know that now. Nothing precious is sacred, not even a childhood. If there's one thing the War of Seven Lambs made abundantly clear it's that.

>>>*...curse to the child slavers and grownups meant to protect us...* <<<

Here, you must become an action figure. Become cruel, become callous or suffer the wrath of the callous and the cruel.

>>>*...who sold us out. Gripped by their greed, warped by hate. Lulled into inaction with the shiny snare traps of tradition, fear, and fascist snake oil salesmen...* <<<

Petals break fast and thorns bleed the breakers.

>>>*...because of you, we are a blink away from extinction. We will not forget...we will not forgive.* <<<

Grow thorns, baby. <<< [END TRANSMISSION]

In the beginning, one of my favorite pastimes was scratching my name across the park.

I liked giving the place secret scars.

I'm not sure why I did this.

Maybe it was my way of offering proof to the world that I'm still here?

If you look really hard, you'll find CODA carved into the side of a roller coaster here, or some split piece of metal there, twisted up into a double helix in an instant by the blast. Check the underside of a railing or find me scrawled across an old flimsy mobile cart where they once kept cold the cartoon popsicles and overpriced bottles of water. Even etched it into the giant memorial bell bearing Mathison Mauswick Jr himself's portrait, having safely unhooked and hidden away the ringer inside. Over 500 times you'll find this, there abouts, graffitied across the park.

I always scratch out the name, though.

I remember reading once that negation is a form of—

*Shhhhhh.*

Do you hear that?

It's definitely real this time.

SOMEbody's coming.

THINGS THE WAR OF SEVEN LAMBS TAUGHT ME:

1.Grow fire in your belly

2.Always braid your bones for battle

*Scabbers.* Four of them. Nothing special. Run-of-the-mill waste trash sniffing for an easy kill.

You can usually tell a scabber by how theatrically adorned they are. They tend to dress like devils, because some people are afraid of that sort of thing I guess. Comics have ruined us all. In this case of this lot, we've got twitch tats, bionic horns, reptile pigmentation tablets, and filed-down shark dentures—the latest in ridiculous scabber fad.

But the ones who look like devils aren't the ones you should be afraid of. They do that because they know they're not long for this world. Know all too well the depths of their own cowardice. They can feel their end coming, fate squeezing in on them like a trigger.

They're nothing like grimers. Grimers actually *ARE* the devil—with their extraction kits slung on their sides ready to gut out your organs for the highest bidder. They'll pluck out your spleen like a lemon seed. I've only heard the occasional tale, but in these tales you never see them coming. Just feel the scalpel sawing through your sternum. Wet squelch of organs and clattering of bone.

"Spread out" says the scabber with a shark's smile, pushing air into words through tiny triangles of teeth. They sound sort of like a talking snake, like Coilee Carl from the early Merrymaus cartoons. "Food firsst, then fun."

Good to see them dividing… saves me the trouble of splitting them up on my own.

I enjoy playing with my prey.

I decided long ago I didn't need anybody else.

My father was a composer. He, like many other "intellectual rats," was one of the first ones out in the streets protesting for my rights, before protesting itself was eventually made illegal.

The regime found efficient ways to dispense with this clamorous lot. First my father lost his job, and then when he spoke out – even louder this time on live television – someone spotted him on TV. Came the flurry of death threats. Came the not-so-discreet invitations to find a new country if he didn't like this one. Then one day came a truck. I'm told he died instantly kissing its bumper, though I suspect this was one of the surgeon's white's lie to offer me some semblance of comfort as a bawling, newly fatherless child.

Soon after that incident, the National Youth Civil Servitude Act was passed, retroactively making all citizens aged 5-15 automatic property of the US military. Children who weren't originally born here – or more aptly, children *perceived* as not having been born here - were immediately shipped overseas for undisclosed "duty".

Children of the rich were initially spared—anyone whose parents could afford the extravagant Patriot Fee for building up the borders. When the poor came for them too though, the law was quickly remedied.

Such madness seems implausible even now, surveying its wreckage. That's exactly what the majority who stood by and let it happen thought, too.

No one ever believes that things can get so bad until they do.

They never believe they can get even worse than that, until they do.

By then, it's always too late.

In the youth battalion, due to my slightly above age intelligence, emotional maturity, and technical proficiency I was made a tinker. This entailed fixing things mostly, taking them apart, and generally getting my hands dirty.

Later on, when the olders learned my penchant for mercilessness, manipulation, and self-survival, I was promoted to a handler.

"Handler" – an elegant euphemism for the grisly business it actually involved: leading the youngest age group, who we all dubbed minecatchers, whose unenviable task it was to wander enemy territory using their bodies to pinpoint the exact location of active mines, to their merry deaths.

Here is a list of other nicknames for handlers:

-Pied Piper

-Dethshepherd

-Grimguide

-Softslayer

-Babykiller

(You would never let the olders hear you uttering such distinctions; illegal terminology and such):

My favorite minecatcher was a boy named Teddy. His story, which is the bigger story of the war, is his own to tell so I'll leave him to tell it in his own way. All you need know is he lived longer than most and seemed oblivious to the many evils his young life had subjected him to up to the very end.

He had been told from the very beginning, like all minecatchers, that heaven was a big playground where your mother would be waiting for you, on the other end of a very long slide that unfurled like a giant's spiral tongue, but only if you were lucky enough to "catch" a mine.

Soon after he did just that, I decided to retire from war.

Bit of advice: don't ever tell anyone you're going AWOL.

Just go.

Merrymausland is divided into four distinct quarters, each with its own theme, attractions, and classic Merrymaus mascot.

The north – The Golden Kingdom - is the domain of the main star, Merry Gold Merrymaus, where the best rides are, or rather where they used to be. That's where Stormer's Cove is, affording a bird's eye view of the whole park. It's also home to remnants of the Infinity Shuttle – a breakneck coaster and all-around favorite, Manic Mangoose's Monstery Manor, and Ninjas of the Orient (yes, really), a dubious indoor flume ride with now foul-smelling, irradiated water and its very own long succession of cinematic adaptations that seemed like they might could go on forever. Let us not forget the oldest ride in the park, the rickety and inadvertently nightmare-inducing It's a Merry Merry Land Ain't It?

To the east is Dandy Lion's Discovery Village, full of thrilling educational attractions like the Obscure Hall of Dignitaries, which families would sometimes slip in just to escape the heat, and Hypertime Moon Safari, which despite the coolness of its name was one of the milder attractions, a slow-as-snails creeping tour of mankind's manifest destiny housed inside an otherwise impressively inverted pyramid. Trust me—it was much more exciting to look at than be inside, back when it was still standing.

To the south is Zinny Yuh's *Neigh*borhood, an anthropomorphized horse who had a pet horse of her own, which never seemed to bother anyone but me I guess. This is where most of the gift shops and restaurants could be found. It's also where they held an ostentatious pop-up parade like clockwork every ten minutes throughout the day, every day except Sunday. Note that the parade took seven minutes to make the rounds around the pavilion, leaving only three minutes for families to frantically vacate the sidewalks before getting stuck there to witness the entire spectacle all over again. Due to large crowds, some families wouldn't make it across without watching the same parade four or five or even six times. The trick was to force them into the shops for all those cheaply-made souvenirs. This trick always worked.

Finally, in the west, where just outside the sprawling gates you'll find a scattering of wending crackodile swamps, marshes, and dimly neon bogs, is Dafty Dill's Kiddy Corner. Dafty Dill was a really dumb wolf who was so bad at being a wolf that he gave up meat and decided to be a candy chef instead. (Imagine a Willy Wonka type except clumsier with patchwork overalls and a hat made out of licorice.) This part of the park was once packed with teeth-rotting concession stands, a fully functional midway, and a few rides for the little ones, including Raddish the Ribbit's Jangly Jaunt, which might as well have been called Projectile Vomit: The Ride.

Come night, I'll count my bullets in peace. Six tall: porcelain-painted, pretty as crackledile teeth.

But in the morning, with the sun slumping its nose up through a slimy gauze of smog, I'll do my rounds.

I have something called musical memory. It's exactly what it sounds like—I remember music the way someone with eidetic memory can recall images, with nearly perfect precision (though the mind is bound to take some liberties, imposing some erroneous variation to keep us guessing—from dying of eventual boredom.)

Due to this condition, rising and falling intonations, instrumental nuance, and the subtle shifts inherent in a melody swim around in the ductwork of my brain as if a record is spinning just behind my eyelids. It's kind of like a jukebox someone carved in my skull; in other words, I never had a pressing need for an iPod.

At the moment, I'm hearing Lovely Day by Bill Withers in all its grandeur. It's always on my mind during these routine perambulations around the perimeter, I think because it was my father's favorite song not of the classical persuasion. I remember it always filling the house when I was kid but only early in the morning. Other parts of the day were strictly reserved for Rachmaninov, Puccini, Mozart, and Copland. All other parts except for the night. The night belonged to Shostakovich and Chopin.

MORNING ROUTINE:

Exterior-

Check Bear Traps [√]

Deadfalls/Clean Out Caught Bodies [√]

Ensure Gate Integrity [√]

Welcome Pikes/Replace If Necessary [√]

Gathering of Bogfruit, Other Edibles From
Crackledile Swamps [√]

Interior-

Sled Any Caught Bodies Inside/Secure [√]

Check Sliding Spring Traps [√]

Scrounge Any Scrap Needed for Repairs [√]

Move Food Cache If Time [√]

*NEW* Check/Feed the Wolfpups

Dear Wolfmother,

Thank you for your teeth. May they serve as whetstones to sharpen the bloodthirsty tongue of my railsword.

A quick update on your babies, which I've decided to name. (I hope you don't mind.)

---

One with the perpetually lolling tongue = Mozart.
Our greying gal, coat full of snow = Tchaikovsky.
Runt of the litter with the broken ear = Beethoven, of course.
And, last but not least, the one with wild shifty eyes and
mange = Ives.

---

So I've been leaving out Merrymausbars and at first they were gobbling them up, starved as they were with their ribs poking through. However, they stopped accepting my gift of half-melty chocolate with terrifying gumball eyes and marshmallow teeth about two weeks ago. Lately, I've been leaving out birds and small rodents snagged in the bear traps. They seem to appreciate these meager offerings.

You may be surprised to learn that Ives has been keeping his own company away from the others. Between you and me, I suspect he will last far longer than the others.

If he hasn't had his fill of crushed bird or rat à la mode he'll sometimes fight the others for theirs, and they seem to always back down. He is smart enough to know not to come anywhere near me, which is a good sign. He knows to stay away from humans. I don't blame him. If he doesn't strike out on his own as a lone wolf, I predict he'll emerge as the alpha?

Beethoven, on the other hand, has come up and sniffed my hand a few times, close enough for me to strike him down. Therefore, I predict he won't last long. Such trust will only get him roasted by scabbers. The other two, Tchaikovsky and Mozart, seem to lag behind, subservient to the others. I'm not sure why.

Anyway, they are all growing at an astounding rate. They still sound like pups though. Their snarls come out in little squeaks, like domesticated dogs of old. Only Ives has dared to bare his fangs at me.

Good boy, I always tell him.

Until next time, be at peace Wolfmother.

-C

You should travel light if you hope to survive here. Here's what I carry on any given day...

-*Z9 Huntress Carbine, with a melted-on pipe scope (lens hand-cut, fitted from the mystic mirror in Monstery Manor) and aluminum echo-softening muter*

-*Claire de Lune, my trusty railsword, whose blade I extracted from a dangling bit of Infinity Shuttle track. Braided onto a hunk of steel from the monorail's bumper and bolted, punched-through with padded leather hilt from a harness I found*

-*Mausenstein, a nightmarish mask stitched together from all of the major Merrymaus mascot's heads. I've found it elicits the perfect cocktail of shock and jangly nerves from uninvited guests. Unless I'm safe at the top of Stormer's Cove or nestled smug in the monorail nest, it's best left on the head. You get used to the heat*

-*Three coals in my left pocket. Though I would never start a fire with them (which are visible miles away—you also get used to semi-raw meat cooked slowly against metal in the sun), you never know when you'll need to create a distraction by throwing something*

...and that's it.

Handful of bullets, lined neatly like soldiers ready to load in and light 'em up from a distance, is all you need.

My favorite composer is Charles Ives. For one, he remains obscure and found little love for his music during his lifetime, which is automatically endearing to me. Secondly, his music was all about individuality – the singular unit acting and reacting to and/or against the collective. It's extraordinarily simple and complex at the same time. Bare bones at first superficial listen but bursting with little secrets, littered with abandon and nuance. You just have to go looking for them. It's also sad, but sad in a comforting way.

My favorite piece of his is entitled The Unanswered Question. In it, strings flutter, swelling, in a void until a horn comes along and posits the meaning of existence. One by one, woodwinds struggle to answer, becoming more and more panicked until they give up, leaving the horn to announce the question one last time only to be met with silence.

To me, this is the most beautiful piece of all time because it's the most honest piece of all time. Not like Bach or Beethoven, whose sonatas, quartets, concertos seemed too ornate. Featured too much instrumentation, with a false elegance I always despised, as if all the people playing those rococo melodies packed into one place could actually emulate such divine harmony. The second they put down those instruments and exited the royal hall, I bet they were back to hating each other. Tearing at each other's pasty skin and powdered white wigs, waving their violas and brandishing their flutes.

Less is more, I say. Their music was also joyful. Painfully joyful.

And I ask you: Of what use is joy now?

♪ Currently playing in my head ♪: Grieg's *In the Hall of the Mountain King.*

Right now I'm quietly setting up a forest of stanchions outside a series of linked souvenir shops called Boomer's Bauble Bazaar in Zinny Yuh's *Neigh*borhood. They're the same brass poles that once kept the crowds from killing each other while waiting to ride the rides, herded like cattle. I've placed them equidistantly apart, one every 8 feet or so, to form a spectacle of small terrors that will greet one of the scabbers once he finishes meandering through, combing the caved-in shelves for scrap. He'll exit right here, where I'll be waiting.

He won't notice me, of course. Not at first, not while wearing Mausenstein, because upon each stanchion I've placed a cartoon mascot head and if I stand still I'll blend right in. At least for long enough to see the look in his eyes when he realizes I'm no cartoon.

These stanchions are the same ones used for the "welcome pikes" outside each of the major gates, except in this case I haven't had time to prepare them for maximum effectiveness. See, the welcome pikes are crucial in warding off nosy transients. They, too, wear mascot masks but there's a special surprise underneath, and it's this surprise that matters most. It's the one that sends the loudest message. To anyone brave enough to lift up a mascot mask - and they always do, except for maybe this dumb bunch - they'll find a human head that once belonged to an intruder like them.

Quick tip: it's 500% more effective if you can make them smile. Sometimes this is as simple as asking someone if they wouldn't mind smiling right before you kill them. (You'd be surprised how many actually agree to this.) Other times, long nails will do the trick after the fact, pinned upward through the cheeks at an angle, to hold the pose. The most ironic thing is the use of ketchup packets to stain their teeth; works better than blood, if you can believe that.

Now a loud clank rattles through the next-to-last shop.

Almost showtime.

This one has the twitch tats. They're little circular razor blades that whirl really fast whenever he flexes. He has some muscle on him, so I chose to take him out first. (Usually it's the smartest one you want to go after first – lop off the head of the beast and the body will usually go limp – but in this case, the leader has shark teeth. You shouldn't judge a book by its cover, I know, but I don't peg this book as anything but a pop-up. Picture book at best.

Here he comes.

Get ready, suckas.

"Alright. You buncha sand-sippin' waistoids. Come on out."

He thinks it's a prank, but I can tell he's not completely sure. He's afraid to move suddenly.

"Come on. You know this ain't any kinda funny. I'm serious now."

Shoulders trembling. He's about to learn I'm serious too.

"GUYS, ENOUG—"

*Swish.*

I wait until he sees me to swing my sword, of course, because savoring it means everything.

And I totally do: the fat pills of his eyes gone dilated, tongue stilled inside his mouth, until it's hanging over his bottom lip like a glob of flattened bubble gum.

The inked discs on his skin rev up really fast for a moment, his bones bracing, before grinding to a dramatic halt.

This one, I'll keep on ice for later.

*One down... Three to go.*

I saw a bird trying to build a home out of frayed wires and assorted trash the other day.

*Too late*, I wanted to scream at it.

There used to be a ride in the Golden Kingdom called Icarus Odyssey. Enormous metal wings would get strapped on to your shoulder blades and you'd go for a ride over the park happily screaming, slung around like a puppet. They tore it down around the same time the war got going.

How did it all happen like it did? you may be wondering. And the answer is shockingly simple: People are quite happy to obey. Most people in this world will always listen to the loudest one in the room. Some crave the craven men who pour poison into their ears, telling them everything is going to be ok, in just the right voice.

*Hush, hush. There, there. I'm here now, and I'm going to fix everything...Make it how it once was when everything was simple. When everything was perfect. Just leave it to me. Rest your troubled heart. O you poor ragged things...*

Orderliness at the expense of humanity—that's what happened. The small-minded preferring the knowns of this life over anything unfamiliar to their last dying breath, even when what's known is savage, inhuman. Amoral and horrifying.

Put differently, shackles can be made to appear as wings and a surprising amount of people won't care to tell the difference. They much prefer the illusion of flight. They'd rather not look down to notice all the necks they've been stepping upon, how the weight on their shoulders shifts, pressed down just enough as to transfer away the burden.

Meanwhile, the sky has been stolen away by madmen with tapeworms for power.

One thing you have to understand: a few years without seeing the sky, you start to forget what stars even look like.

I still believe there's love in the world.

It's just not here.

♪ Currently playing ♪: Camille Saint-Saëns' *Danse Macabre.*

Bionic horns are a relatively inexpensive procedure here in the Scorch, though prone to infection. All it takes is cutting a bit of skin near the temples and implanting a pair of cheap chips with retractable prongs, around which a shell of outer skin will eventually regrow, scarified to lend the horns an even gnalier visage.

At the moment, I'm watching a scabber with what looks to be an exceptionally shoddy job – one side shiny with puss, definitely infected – who thinks they're getting the jump on me.

They're not.

Skulking low to the ground, their grip high on their machete's hilt, they've been tracing a pair of watermarked footprints to one of only two access points left that lead to the hunted tunnels underground. What they're too stupid to realize is I painted on these footprints myself, and the junk strategically placed around the access point conceals a secret ramp with a very hair-trigger spring trap.

They won't realize until it's too late. Until they're lowering themselves into the platform, sliding open the cover, and stepping one foot down the sloped slab of pavement. Until their ankle gently tickles a cord to release an avalanche of trash behind them, plugging up the exit and sealing them in indefinitely.

There are no lights down there, except for one spot where a high grate with several slats allows in some natural sunlight during the daytime. The rest of it is one big labyrinth. Proper labyrinth for a proper minotaur.

When the park was still functioning, these tunnels were employees-only, housing various offices and security hubs, break rooms and changing rooms where mascot actors on their breaks would sit around shuffling cards or grabbing a shower. When I first came here I spent weeks exploring its depths (with light, of course, compliments of a seemingly endless supply of glow-in-the dark toy swords). Even though it was the only place that scared me in the entire park, I explored it until it scared me no longer, until I had memorized every inch of its innards. Now I know these corridors like the back of my hand. I even have a number of saferooms where I keep food caches now, hidden so well that nobody who isn't already looking for them will find them.

The only other access point is a deep chamber where I dump my growing collection of trespassers. At this point it stinks something fierce, even with a series of tarps over it.

You get used to the stench of the dead, same as you do the living.

One day, perhaps not too far off, I'll add this scabber to the pile but not until they've run themselves ragged through the darkness for several days first. When they're too weak to even lift that machete, I'll pop down and pay them a visit. I've left them a single glow sword with a battery that's nearly depleted. (One shouldn't lose their sense of humor, even in the middle of the apocalypse.)

I'm not even looking when I hear the spring trap bolt and hear the subsequent ruckus: a faint scream smothered by an explosion. Cascade of debris.

If you're wondering what haunts the haunted tunnels, it's me.

I'm the minotaur.

*Two down.*

My father once told me that the symphony of the universe is hopelessly out of tune.

At the time, he failed to also mention how the sheet music was written upside-down, that all the instruments were made of knives and the stage was quicksand and the conductor was armless and the concert walls were on fire while the audience sat facing backwards.

I suppose even a symphony out of tune is still music . . .

In the very center of the park where all the quarters converge there's this carousel.

In the center of this carousel, there is a spinning orange tycoon named Lord Mudpant. In the old Merrymaus cartoons he was always trying to trick the others into investing in a railroad that led to nowhere, trying to collect their signatures on a comically long contract. He rode around in a diamond-studded hot-air balloon like the Wizard of Oz. (They were fake diamonds, of course; sometimes you'd see him slapping them on like stickers or peeling them off.) He powered the balloon himself, no fire to speak of; he simply exhaled hot air with such force that he could blow himself any which direction for miles, to his and others' perilous and merry whim.

Adults always liked Lord Mudpant but children never did. We could always see through him, see his end game. He wasn't whimsical or funny, just sad and tragic. But he was scary too. Maybe that's why they finally decided to get rid of him. He was never meant to be a villain, just a bumbling clown.

Nevermind that cartoons couldn't die. If they could have, his unfinished railroad would have been the end of them all—the whole Merrymaus extended family.

In my opinion, clowns are the most dangerous of all because no one ever takes them seriously. Everyone's so busy laughing at them they don't realize the clown's not laughing. He actually means to murder someone with that banana peel.

The point is, this carousel never made sense to me. The once vibrant, brightly-colored Merrymaus classic characters that you could ride around on the revolving platform, high-build and saddled and impaled through with twirling poles, all look tired and desperate to stop. All chipped and peeling now. In time, it's like they're still turning, but that's only a nostalgic longing for yesteryear's lies.

And Lord Mudpant still presides in the middle, standing tall, coat of orange paint fresh as ever. His long contract flows down to the floor, crowded with cursive signatures, penned in ink red and ripe as blood. He is grinning, always, grinning like Mephistopheles and the carnival music need not even be playing to hear it in your head.

Everything is eternally revolving around him, and he has already won.

♪ Currently playing ♪: Prokofiev's *Peter and The Wolf March*.

I've been shadowing Shark Teeth for sixty-three steps now. (The trick is to step only when they step, but make sure the sun isn't behind you. Patience is key. Don't ever get too giddy. Time your moving to coincide with their every pivot or lurch. Wait until their guard's down to pounce.)

Shark Teeth is a skinny thing, gaunt and famished by how taut his pale skin looks stretched over his bones. His mohawk rippling with streaks of purple. I can hear him licking his parched lips as he approaches Tchaikovsky, who is currently lounging in the shade of a smashed ATM licking her hindparts.

She doesn't know to be scared, and the drooling scabber can practically already taste the barbecue wolfchops on his tongue.

"C'mere volfy volfy volfy," he hisses high, slicing a meat cleaver through the air as a whistle slips through the gaps of those ridiculous slivered baby fangs. Tchaikovsky rolls over, oblivious. Unimpressed and unintimidated.

The lone scabber hangs his blade over the snowy pup's fur and for the first time since the scabbers' arrival now I remove my mask, chunking it wide right. Watching Shark Teeth watching it roll. (It is then I catch the snatch of grey in my locks—a rogue strand I'll be sure to excise later like the cancerous tumor it is.)

He is slow to turn (he, like the wolf, oblivious), but when he does a mild laugh rises up through his throat. Scratchy little cackle that slips out as he's wiping snot from his nose. "Well isn't this just the Island of Pups...what have we 'ere?" Again he's tracing that rusty cleaver through the air, heavily forming figure 8s. "I didn't think there were any of you left. More meat for us, 'ey?" He flashes that jagmouth at me, trying to wield what might pass for others as a disconcerting, pulse-quickening countenance. "Whadya say, child—you wanna keep me warm tonight?"

Now I lift up the spittoon I've been lugging along. Prop ripped from Stormer's Cove, filled to the halfway mark and sloshing with dark liquid. I sling it back before heaving it forward, drenching the baffled scabber.

"Sure," I agree to his proposal.

It's a few seconds before he can smell it. By it, I mean fate.

"Goodbye, Shark Teeth."

Then, it's as if the lighter magnetizes directly from my palm to his as he attempts to block what's inevitable. I watch him dripping liquid skin, melting in front of me. I do not move. I do not budge. Do not blink. Just watch those flames dancing—a hundred wild tongues licking while his face bubbles, grisly goo oozing from socket and nostril.

Charred flesh smells a bit like a cookout, as one might expect, but also reeks of metal and must. Semi-coppery, with a sweet, acidic tang.

Which is to say, his head is one that won't make it to the welcome pikes.

At least Tchaikovsky has the good sense to find a new spot now. She shimmies away, tail tucked between her legs, wearing a faint dusting of ash over her silvery pelt.

*Three down... One left.*

Here in Merrymouseland, the rain smells of uranium. I'm not sure what that smells like exactly, but I imagine the rain is still heavily irradiated so that's why I say it. At least I know if it gets in your eyes it'll sting for a few minutes. If you leave it there longer, you'll go blind. If it gets in your mouth, you'll either puke sporadically, off and on for months, or die on the spot. If it kisses your skin, that skin will turn a bluish-green like molded bread. I've heard of it infecting people in all kinds of weird ways, too—growing hair there that's not their natural color. Sprouting a spiral maw of external teeth on the elbow. I once even heard of someone with a mushroom blooming thick from within the cave of their belly button. (This one, I doubt. . . I mean, who could be so lucky? Mushrooms are a rare treat.)

In other words, it's the worst kind of lottery.

It occasionally looks beautiful though, in the right sunset, needling down with that luminescent glint, especially scenic from the monorail nest—my second favorite perch in all of Merrymouseland. Sitting high atop a precarious twist of track outlooking the crackodile swamps,  inside a single monorail cart that's been bashed in like a sardine tin, it's difficult to access. To get there, I utilize a simple weight/counter-weight system: a pulley with a single foothold that I ride to the top and then pull up once there. It's my exact weight, so for anyone else it will either immediately snap or will fail to lift them. While Stormer's Cove is still the prime perch for the view it affords one of the entire park, the monorail nest often feels safer. Hidden and secret, a pocket of fresh sanctuary tucked away, if such a thing can even exist here.

It's where I sit now, sewing sutures into Mausenstein and watching the wolfpups down below, licking up puddles of rainwater. (♪ Currently playing ♪: Erik Satie's *Gymnopédie No.1*)

Ives is the only one with enough sense to know this is bad for him, and I fear that the other three wolfpups aren't cut out for this world. Maybe they'll learn, but I doubt it.

There may come a point when something might need to be done about that?

By which I mean: Some animals kill their young when those young are sick or extraordinarily weak.

It's survival of the fittest, I know, but I like to think mercy is also in there somewhere... an equally important part of a seemingly macabre equation.

If you pray to the rain, saying just the right words in just the right order, with your hands clasped accordingly and your head bowed not too high and not too low, do you think will it bring you people? I wonder this briefly now before dismissing it, just as quick as a fork of lightning thrashes through a blue ache of sky. Forget it; whatever. I'm not the praying type and would surely mess it up. Hope has nothing to do with the rain, anyway... merely the hint of rain. The fine mist of maybe. I don't know what I'm saying.

I sit reading an old employee's manual.

Chapter One: How to Be Merry All the Time. Chapter Two: How to Maintain Order. Chapter Three: How to Casually Avert Catastrophe. Chapter Four: Smile! Chapter Five: A Note on Queue Control. Chapter Six: Steering Them Toward the Shops. Chapter Seven: Further Notes on Queue Control. Chapter Eight: Safety and Litigation Practices. Chapter Nine: Merriness is a State of Mind. Chapter Ten: Additional Reading and Useful Strategies for Queue Control.

It doesn't matter what the ride is, as long as there are orderly queues with pretty ropes to herd you along. The ride could be a meat grinder for babies but as long as there are orderly queues with pretty ropes to wait in, people won't panic. *Surely*—they'll say to themselves, rubbing their panicked hands over the braided velvet and velour—*surely there's someone in charge here?*

♪ Currently playing ♪: Julius Fucik's *Entry Of The Gladiators*

Presently, I've got my barrel poked through a crack in the monorail nest's window resting, aim traced on Reptile Skin, who's been trudging through hip-high mud in the crackodile swamps. It keeps getting higher, and he's starting to panic now. When he came upon what remained of Shark Teeth – in all his contorted crispiness – he bolted for the west gate.

Reptile pigmentation tablets are a thrifty substitute for semi-serviceable armor in the Scorch. They gnarl the skin into hideous knots, scabbing into a nearly impenetrable patch but only for a few hours. When it wears off, the skin is twice as vulnerable so it's definitely a trade-off.

This poor scabber's purchase wore off about ten minutes ago, and even from miles off I can see him wincing pronouncedly, as the bogthorns lash and scrape at his exposed arms. He's slowing, the fatigue weighing him down, legs going leaden. I can see those albino bumps in the water beginning to circle, too.

He'll be dead by the time the moon crests and Merrymouseland will be safe once more. Pure, at least for a spell, until the next clueless encroachers step foot on my domain and it's time to go to work again.

I pull my barrel out of the window slit to let nature take its course.

There was a time when I would've donated a bullet to him to spare him the indignity of being eaten alive.

That time is known as ancient history.

In the war, we learned to scorn the youngers just as the olders learned to scorn us. Learned to treat the youngers as disposable just as the olders learned to treat us as disposable. In other words, we inherited our hate by watching, learning, doing. Until it came natural, and it was like breathing. Until we wore our cruelty like a second skin.

Questioning the order of things—uttering *why?* was the greatest sin. So, we learned to exile this word from our vocabularies early on, banishing the inclination to ask. Like stones swallowed, that would sink and stay sunken in the lakes of our bellies.

Don't let anyone tell you otherwise: The world exists to break your heart.

Some deal with this fact by breaking it back. Others just end up breaking themselves.

A few, who are somehow able to accept what's broken, may find a way to be grateful for it.

These people are called fools.

You can tell a lot about a person by how they bleed.

"Do you know of Procrustes?"

I watch the first scabber again, the one with twitch tats, as his pupils widen in recognition of my voice. Head wagging; I take that as a no.

"He's from Greek mythology. My third favorite next to Prometheus and Medusa."

His eyes search his surroundings, noticing the darkening sky over him. Feeling cold steel on his spine.

"He lived in a fortress near a mountain pass that he would lull travelers into. Invite them to sleep in a very special bed. Like the most perfect host."

Right about now he's probably wondering why he can't turn his head. Why his extremities aren't tingling. The first one is easy: I've tied it down.

"The thing is, he wanted the bed to be perfect for his guests. He'd go to great lengths to accomplish this."

As for the second one. *Well...*

"If they were too short or too small, he'd stretch their body until it fit. On the other hand, if they were too tall or wide, their limbs dangling off the edge even the slightest bit, he'd cut them right off."

Now comes the primal scream. Enough to rattle the loosening metal behind his neckskin.

I remove the tie-down around his head to allow him to see my project now—how I've fastened him to the track of the roller coaster. One-size-fits-all, with just one surgically precise railsword swipe. The legs I've spared. He won't need them too much longer, anyway.

"Ple-please. I'll leave and never come back," he pleads, as they all do eventually. Lying, as they all do.

"How many scabbers do you think have told me that, only to come back with their friends later?"

He thinks it a trick question, and it is. He's calculating something in his head, adding up the hard facts.

"Zero," he finally answers with a fatal sigh.

Ding-ding-ding. It's the right answer, but it won't save him.

As I softly nod, I can tell he has embraced his fate.

"You were in the war weren't you?"

Another nod. His eyes stabbing at me wild for a second, before his whole aura seems to

go cold. Sober though not quite serene.

"Then it doesn't matter what I say to you does it?"

I'd tell him it's not personal but I'm sure he knows this already.

The Law of the Scorch is unwritten because everyone still alive knows it. It might as well be written in blowtorch and blood. It's the reason so many clan up to increase their odds. Survival is the only rule – alpha and omega - and one warm body out there left alive means one more body left running around likely to leave yours cold later.

At this point, I respect his acceptance of his own crummy luck. Of all the amusement parks in all the world, he had to walk into this one. Call it a bad draw of the cosmic deck.

Because of this, I pull the crank now to tip the cart at the top of the track. It'll be quick. He'll hear it rumble and then he won't hear anything at all.

I don't even ask him to smile. He's earned the right to frown. To glower and grimace, gnash his teeth and curse his fate if he wants.

Only true warriors are deserving of this privilege.

Dear Wolfmother,

Thank you for your meat. It bears your same sweetness and fullness of spirit, and though they've licked their lips at the sight of my consumption of you, I have obviously not shared any with your children. That would be...well, I wouldn't do that.

However, it's on the subject of them that I write you now, with great concern. And I must warn you that these words of mine may bring you pain, but I pray that if you are in disagreement you will relay to me a sign – I only ask that it not be too vague - in all of your infinite wisdom.

Here it is: With the exception of Ives, I fear the worst for your wolfpups. Given this grim world, its numerous elements both natural and unnatural, I marvel honestly that they have made it this far.

The evidence of late has been piling that some gesture of mercy is what's required of me, because I would rather see them put down with grace than flayed by scabbers. Again, it is not my wish to cause you any distress beyond the grave, so I ask again if you have objections to make them known in whatever manner you may, within the next few days.

I will be listening solemnly. If silence prevails, I will ready my methods and do my service. If, on the other hand, word is received via wind, some cosmic sign or whatever, I am keen to alter my plans.

I am certain you are missing your ilk and may even harbor secret hopes of an early reunification, in which case I am happy to oblige.

Whatever the case may be, please consider my plans and let me know your thoughts.

-C

Dear Wolfmother,

Three days have lapsed into three weeks. Three weeks into three months . . .

The wolves may be growing but all of them, except Ives, who snaps healthily at me from a distance with brooding eyes, remain soft still.

Their sinewy muscles and broad jaws betray them.

I have heard only silence.

It is time.

Forgive me.

-C

Beneath the wreckage of an old float I can see Ives, watching me now with his tilting skeptic head. He knows something is up, which is more than I can say for Mozart, Tchaikovsky, and Beethoven, who came at first call. Their trust of me, built carefully over time with a steady supply of easy nourishment, will be the end of them. They should know by now nothing good is easy here. Though their bodies – at least the two of them - are no longer prototypically lean like wolfpups, they still think like wolfpups. Only Ives is shapely, with a brutish mass that tells me he's been finding meat on his own, sneaking outside the gates to venture solo at night.

I have chosen the courtyard outside Manic Mangoose's Monstery Manor because it feels somehow fitting, funereal with its picturesque fountains, Styrofoam tombstones, and shrubbery once so immaculately pruned every morning. Now, it conveys a wildness that is both ordinary and sacred.

I keep thinking: were I a wolf no longer wild, would I mind dying here?

It is Beethoven who has presented himself openly to me, boldly even, while Mozart and Tchaikovsky stare on, wondering why I've summoned them all here. So it is Beethoven I'll do first; the other two will be easy enough to catch later on, if they even have the good sense to flee.

"Right here, boy," I chirrup. Oblivious, the omega of the pack rests on his haunches where I've knelt before him, one broken ear folded over. He's scrawny, ribs like sticks stabbing out from tender leaves. He's been slowest to the scraps and you can tell.

"Stupid boy," I go to graze his head, and to my surprise he allows it, even leaning in with half-shut eyes. It's as if he needs it or something – contact, touch, whatever – and that more than anything else is why he has to be the first to go.

Without warning I lift high my railsword.

Don't blink.

There's really no need to drag this out, is there?

He is still patient on his haunches. Still waiting. Stupid, stupid boy.

I never notice the weight of my unconventional blade but I'm noticing it now; I've done this so many times in the war, basically the same thing, and never once did I feel the weight of it.

Don't blink.

He's not opening his eyes back up fully and something about this bothers me.

Everything is heavy now and I don't know why.

"Open your eyes," I shout down at him. He only crosses his paws, waiting still.

Stupid, stupid boy.

One mustn't permit such hesitations.

"Open. Your. Eyes." They seem to close even wider now just to spite me, head falling into the lattice of his paws. He pants, but it's not a nervous pant. It's obsequious—slow with deferent exhales. Big dumb domesticated breaths.

Dontblink.

"Open your eyes!"

He is weak and by every natural law of the universe he deserves to be punished for this.

He *deserves* it… but for the life of me I can't bring myself to drop the guillotine.

Don'tblink.

Finally his eyes pop open. twinkling, low-lit with something long forgotten. Something I'd rather stay forgotten – entombed with a long history of looks – but there is no unseeing what's been seen, just like there is no unfeeling what's been felt.

Don'tblink

*Stupid. You're so stupid…*

He is weak, and I can't bring myself to end him because I am weak too.

New plan: I have lured all four wolfpups down into the haunted tunnels.

When it came to Ives I almost threw in the towel. You could see the balls behind his eyes whirling, working hard, calculating and successfully chalking it up to the trap that it was. He knew better, but in the end he couldn't refuse the quality chum, compliments of our friend Twitch Tat.

The other three basically dove in on their own accord, knowing nothing of the darkness and what lies below. I figure they'll be safe here from the outside world unless the outside world finds them first, which it won't unless something happens to me. Maybe down there they'll grow stronger, mean enough to make it for the long haul?

It's mostly the other three I'm worried about, of course. I'm hoping Ives will teach them a thing or two about how the world works. About humans and hunting and what you must do to survive.

I've even provided them with some prey to practice on.

I never appreciated the Obscure Hall of Dignitaries until the end of the world.

Very often now, I find myself sitting here in the front row of plush theatre seating, having hand cranked just enough low-crackling voltage to provide a banal show featuring animatronic orators speaking very slowly about the modern definition of liberty.

The same show that used to make me fall asleep as a kid still almost does sometimes, like a long-forgotten lullaby.

Mostly I don't even hear the words though, anymore. I intentionally tune them out, remembering instead a heartbreaking song. (♪ Currently playing ♪: *O Mia Babbino Caro*, performed by Maria Callas and written by Giacomo Puccini...)

Don't think I'm missing much. The words of the show aren't applicable anymore.

I'm just here for the beautiful backdrop: a room full of pretend people.

It's the only time I'd risk having my back to a door.

I wear 3-D shades and wishing for popcorn.

I don't really know why I'm here.

I don't know why I'm weeping.

Rearming the spring trap that seals shut the main access port to the haunted tunnels is a bit of a chore. Clearing the trash is the easy part, thanks to a combination winch/heavy net system I designed myself that does most of the work for me. This was done with the simple press of a button over a week ago when I relocated the wolfpups; it's kind of like one big claw machine game.

No, it's getting the big metal freezer that rolls down along the ramp to trigger the whole chain reaction that's the hard part. I've been holding off on doing it until it's cooler because it's ungodly heavy... it'll slide when you least expect it and the last thing I need is a broken foot.

In the old world, a broken foot might have meant a cast or a crutch. Here, it is a guaranteed death sentence.

The last few days have been sweltering and the heatwave doesn't look like it'll break anytime soon though, so I figure I might as well get it done.

I've got it about halfway up the ramp with the help of a metal pipe I've sawed slantwise to give me some leverage when I witness a single droplet of sweat dripping from my forehead. It plinks perfectly between the web of my thumb and index, in grueling slow motion. It's almost cliché, like something from a cartoon, and this fact elicits an immediate yowl of laughter.

What follows next is predictable—a perfect tsunami of dominoes. There's my left hand slipping. There's me, rolling backwards like a human snowball. There's the monster of the freezer following after, and then me pitching myself down into the mouth of the haunted tunnels to avoid getting kamikaze crushed. Finally, there's me splayed out on the damp anteroom floor, looking up at a ring of dusty daylight. I'm pretty sure there's a bone sticking out of my leg too, just above my kneecap.

Once my heart is done thumping like a drum wound so tight it could burst, I'm sure the pain will kick in.

But then there is a vague sniffing behind me. Curious shuffling of fur just beyond the perceptible edges in the darkness. Breath stinking as it rustles forth, poking its nose into the light.

Ives? *Good boy.*

Now the pain is presenting itself, and I can feel that my knee is wet with red. Growing slicker by the second, warm with a steady, even gush.

Ives can sense this too, his head fully exposed now along with fangs fully borne. His mane marbled red just like his teeth. I know right away that he has found my treasure trove of corpses. His eyes are singing now with disgust, and I dare not patronize him by attempting to pacify him with a soothing tone. He is beyond all this, and I am proud of him for it.

His transformation to alpha is complete.

(NOTE TO SELF: Accept now and forever... death begets death and blood only more blood, but hate is also the only thing powerful enough to keep you alive.)

At this point I close my eyes to let the hunter claim his trophy. Let him lunge and be done with me already.

I'm don't expect the snarling hunter's whimper, something snagging at its throat roared out of the darkness.

Once, twice, three times it fends him off.

It's... Beethoven?

Yes, Beethoven. He is standing guard at my feet now, positioning himself between me and Ives. The other two soon reveal themselves as well, frozen in place as if they don't quite know who to side with yet. They're trying to make their minds up still.

Beethoven continues to growl—something much deeper than I would expect. Fiercer.

Though he is much smaller than the other three, his shadow looms larger on the walls.

Ives tries one more time to strike, but the runt of the litter lashes him with a paw and he is done. He cowers at last, and it decided—Beethoven is now the alpha.

It is decided for Mozart and Tchaikovsky, too. They soon join their pack leader on the other side, where they form a semicircle of protection around me.

I try to raise up but flinch in agony.

Before passing out, I can feel Beethoven licking at my wounds.

It feels... clean.

Dear Wolfmother,

I was wrong.

Maybe it's not too late?

-C

Upon waking, the first thing I decide is it's best not to move for now or anytime soon.

I manage to start a small fire, those coals in my pockets finally given some use.

I am willing to risk this light, and soon, wearing a tourniquet fashioned from some trash, I think I'll wait out the sunrise with my new kindred.

Civilization is a sham; it has always been so. Pain is painful; it has always been so. Even at its most beautiful, sunset is only a prelude to night; it has always been so. You were born alone and you'll likely go out the same way; it has always been so. This world was handmade for hate; it has always been so. But none of this make it natural. By which I mean, maybe what's out there doesn't have to be what's in here, between where the heart beats and the brain buzzes. Maybe there's more to the idea of survival than the ripsaw sound of skin cutting, and what we perceive as soft is the only thing worth saving in the end. Is true death something that happens while you're still alive—a kind of preemptive rigor mortis of the soul?

Which is to say, don't catch cold.

Stars wink, embers flash.

Together, me and my wolves bask in their broken afterglow, backs stitched shivering to a cold floor—the makeshift sewer our pillow.

We, the still living, despite all the darkness dancing.

We, the still alive.

Single knot of skin and fur to keep us warm—

Centrifugal

# ADAGIO /// AUTUMN

---

Sometimes I swear I hear somebody scratching on the walls down here.

I fear the worst: Grimer. I turn to find only Ives—pawing, restless, bloodthirsty.

It is Beethoven who keeps him at bay. Always Beethoven.

The other two have sweetened some but you can tell they're constantly waiting for the balance to shift. For the alpha to show some momentary lapse in weakness, or get sick and leave me unguarded for a jot. The scales of collective survival are perpetually tipped in a sliding state.

Luckily for me, and I'm not sure why, Beethoven never leaves my side. Even when he steps away to squirt a smear of yellow on the wall, he has his eyes leveled on his kind the whole time, as if to warn: *The dainty human is not to be touched.*

Make no mistake, tourist: Every story is a/an ______________ story.

A)apocalypse

B)mystery

C)horror

D)revenge

At night, I can feel his furry spine blanketing my belly, chin flat on the floor with one eye squared, hard-squinting. I watch it flicker, flirting with sleep but he is the lightest of sleepers for my protection. He only ever leaves when his brothers and lone sister excuse themselves to feed off the dead that I have stacked like so many planks on the far side of the tunnels. He is quick about this, always careful to return before they do, hustling from one of the human food caches I hid down here for a rainy day. They're all pretty rainy now, I admit, said as my leg continues to leak a viscous red.

I pluck my manufactured meal from his jaws, not minding the drool so much anymore, with a heartfelt thank you. He does his little bow, lowering his eyes and dropping his tongue out of his wide mouth with that dopey pant, and then I remind myself: I am only alive because this wolf allows it.

I wonder if he reminds himself too: I am only alive because this human once allowed it.

And then I wonder if he, like I do sometimes, wonders why each of us prolonged the life of the other, under the circumstances.

Thought echo pinging: I wonder if that old harpoon at the top of Stormer's Cove fires?

Just buying time, the lot of us.

♪ Currently playing ♪: Gustav Holst's *The Planets, Venus*

Dead leaves scrape in through the open mouth of the tunnel and I imagine all the death-things going on aboveground. All that untrammeled chaos in my absence.

Yet I don't *feel* death, not at the moment. I look at Beethoven with his tail tangled around my wrist and feel something else, more like the fleeting wingbeat of hummingbirds. Something oddly sustaining, quickening, lifting, rising through the throat like an invisible voice.

I dare not sing, but I understand what it means and why one would do it. Perhaps it's only the secret urge to scream, and perhaps there isn't much difference between singing and screaming in the end and that's what a howl is—a perfect blend of both.

Then again, maybe I'm just growing soft?

~~When the moon is big like a sinking ship in the sky, glimpsed just so through the perfect corona of the tunnel, we'll still howl out together sometimes, the wolves and I.~~

~~Down here, I think I might actually regain my strength if Ives doesn't win over the others. His howl so different, guttural with menace. When he howls out, it's as if he's worshipping~~

~~not the light of the moon but the carbon black that always threaten to swallow it whole, mad-still and ragged and furtive at its weary edges.~~

Wolf gas is particularly potent. Choke-inducing and cabbage-sour. The long night full of timpani butt blasts strong enough to strip the hairs off inside one's nostrils.

It's all those cadavers they eat, I think?

An odorous chorus that hangs over the tunnels like an albatross of pink puckered, foul-assed demons.

~~Cindered leaves float in, float out. I crunch them in my hand to give my idle hate something to do.     In, out.     The leaves twirling and I find my hands are shaking, whole months hiccupping by until I am sure my beloved kingdom has forgotten all about me.~~

~~There is only one way to find out, I suppose?~~

Having wandered the tunnels for weeks now in preparation, slowly building my strength and shaking off the atrophy, I'm getting ready to venture out again. Beethoven has been at my heel every hobble-step of the way, so assiduous in his concern. A battery-depleted glow sword makes a surprisingly serviceable cane, flashing in the black like an echo of time.

When I reach the surface I squint staring crooked at the lopsided sun, blurry through bricolage tracks before calling down to my kindred to join me.

I half-expected to find the whole place run amok with scabbers, waiting for my coronation ascension, but only dead wind whistles back. I wheeze, moaning under a jigsaw configuration of clouds.

My kindred are slow to come, but when they reach the edge of the light they slink back

down into the tunnels entirely.

"Come on… it's safe now."

A few listless whines and I know something is wrong. It is Beethoven making this call, barring the others outright from crossing into the light. The others trust his decision, and soon they are filing back down with those big clopping paws of theirs. Even Ives accepts the wisdom of this verdict without much fuss.

Beethoven's eyes shine at me through the dark as he bows one last time, and I bow back to my only friend in the world before tearing myself from the tunnels.

With a few parting pants, he joins his brothers and sister in the long dark, and I am once again alone and that is that. I draw Clair de Lune for the first time in a season, trying to will my bones to toughen as I toss that flimsy glow sword to the ground.

Tomorrow, I will venture out and slaughter any scabbers caught on my property. Reestablish dominance & pay whatever blood tithes I owe to buy back order here.

Dear Beethoven,

I don't blame you.

When you grow up in the sewers, I guess it's only a matter of time until you think you belong there. That it is your one true home.

The filth we inherit eventually becomes the filth we feel you deserve.

-C

By the time the War of Seven Lambs was done, over 97% of the world's children were extinct. Children, for whom there was no utilitarian value left in society. Most of these small bodies perished at the hands of each other, made to slaughter the enemy like toy soldiers in one big game of vile chess arranged by the elders.

The few spared from the battlefields ended up in "Dullhouses"—large estates where their minds could be made into mush to better serve their heritors, their rightful legal owner. Millionaires and billionaires would buy up kids by the dozen and relocate them to their lavish mansions, where they would begin their servitude. These chosen few were

~~carefully maintained and monitored. Very few were prone to escaping, finding clever ways to circumvent the nocturnal neurococktails that would render them docile.~~

Thus, the grimer was born: a niche vocation specifically purposed for fetching escaped dulls and/or locating replacement organs for those still in operation.

Grimers make a pretty living, and do so by building clean reputations as impeccable, efficient killers and collectors of spare child parts.

As pretty a living as you can make in such an ugly place.

Absolutely nothing has made its home here in my absence and that's somewhat surprising. Disappointing. Doesn't stop my hand from twitching.

Empty. My kingdom remains empty.

From Stormer's Cove, (27 minutes 10 seconds to reach the top on my one lame leg now) the park looks eerily peaceful. Even the crackledile swamps look placid. A few mustard-colored trees offering zero signs of the skeletal buzzards; no lumps lurking in the sienna moss. The sludge puddles aren't bubbling like usual.

My eyes scan the horizon again for scabbers. Wishful, drunken, desperate.

Something, anything to add to my underground altar.

Little tremors that race through ruddy veins, jostling my hand for a fix.

The first time my hand felt such an unnatural rush I had just disappeared a boy three years my junior. Orders were barked in my direction but that's no excuse. He fell tumbling down a hill and I didn't even blink. When he splashed into a creek at the base, I didn't even blink.

I was given a brand-new tally patch for this, basically a point for the home team.

*Home* team, as if the idea of home could mean anything anymore.

In the intervening years, I have been trying to teach myself how to blink again.

Spying a lump, my fingers drag down huntress with a frenzy. Socket swallowing scope, my itchy index now belongs to an alien hand tugging back the trigger, as buzzards I didn't see before explode out of their autumnal boughs, their movement reminding me of mechanical wind-up toys.

Suddenly my heart is turbopumping and the air is electric, laced with the sweet pinch of gunpowder.

I immediately lament the unnecessary expenditure of a bullet.

The crackodile wasn't even close to the gate. No threat was imminent. Such sloppiness can't be excused.

I don't know why I did it.

At least I pretend not to know.

The hand is my own.

But when I reach the felled mutant it's not the only prize I find.

THINGS THE WAR OF SEVEN LAMBS TAUGHT ME:

1.A baby corpse facedown in the mud can easily be mistaken for an infant animal. Every curvature of ribs is approximately the same: a cage delicately designed to house something soft and seemingly incorruptible.

That same night I drag the sacrificial crackodile out of the shallow radiant muck. It's hell to move, and by the time I have its cumbersome bloated body rolled every nerve fiber of mine is burning.

Right outside the west gate is where I bury both the white-bellied beast and the bones without a name, saying the only prayer I've ever known, which I only heard once and not so clearly at my mom's funeral. (Humanmother, not Wolfmother mind you.)

I hope they will forgive me my mangled words; it's not the words that matter anyway, it's the way you speak them.

*Our father who art somewhere, hollowed be thy name. Thy kingdom crumb, thy will be dumb, on earth as anywhere else. Give us some moldy bread and forgive us our terrible truths. Lead us not into temptation and deliver us from...eagles? Something. Whatever.     Afuckingmen.*

I wish I could crawl back into the underground and sleep again with my kindred, just for tonight, but I know this is forbidden.

I must respect their territory now, just as they must respect mine. As Zeus respected Hades: Mount Olympus and the Underworld co-existing in contrapuntal harmony.

I can't stop thinking of those bones, though. The wind carries a whisper and I imagine all the names that might've belonged to them.

The moon is so high tonight.

Night smeared with neon scabs.

Every bright thing I eventually hate.

If I could fold the sky in half and pocket all these secondhand stars I would.

Damn the light. Damn the chandeliers. Damn their brazen brightnesses. Damn every winged thing and whatever floats adrift through the rust-ridden seas. Damn the ash-capped mountains and flooded valleys. Damn all the cathedrals, still standing with their stain glass mockeries. Damn the steeples and splintered pews. Damn the holy books and crumbling hymnals. Damn the hallelujahs. Damn the sculpted fountains and festering waters. Damn what's left of the regime too, safe behind their ironclad curtains while the rest of the world sinks into oblivion. Damn the atomic roses—cherry-red shrapnel, sobering evidence of the chain blasts that boomed us back into another century. Damn the mutated wild horses. Damn the trampled fields and meadows once meant for galloping. Damn the puttering three-eyed frogs, slapping through their glowing puddles. Damn the dingy strip malls collecting dust. Damn the registers and rustling paper money and loudly clacking coins. Damn the aisles that still stand like exhibits in a haunted museum, their foreign artifacts immaculate. Damn the cars and trucks and luxury SUVs stranded on the highways, trunks popped like eyes winking wide. Damn the lawnmowers left sprawled on their sides in the neighborhoods. Damn the fences. Damn the doors.

Damn the windows half cracked and fly-magnet pies on the sills gathering mold. Damn the manicured gardens. Damn the orchards. Damn the bright tubes and computers, every screen for not being a mirror. Damn the playgrounds, the monkey bars and make-believe fortresses. Damn the schools. Damn the libraries and big oak counters and perfumed books, from which we learned nothing. Damn the movie theaters and gallon buckets of popcorn pumped with rivers of liquid butter. Damn the teeth-corroding sodas. Damn the ripped ticket stubs and previews which were always better than the movies and the entire business of escapism. Damn the upscale restaurants with their fancy linens and gleaming platters. Damn the finely polished silverware and never-sharp-enough cutlery. Damn the glossy, oversized menus. Damn the dumpsters. Damn the sinks. Damn the pipes, bricks, mortar and stone. Damn the walls. Damn the damns. Damn them and damn us, damn me and damn you too. And damn the rainbows. And damn the rainbows. And damn the rainbows. Damn every color that dares to be anything but gray.

I decided to name the bones Emilia.

♪ Currently playing ♪: Antonio Vivaldi's *Storm*

A few days later I am greeted by a storm, brief but bright with furious winds and lashing rain. The kind that blows in crooked to sting shut the eyes. Enough to soak one's clothes to a second skin.

It is everything I can do to seek shelter. When the toxic sands get stirred, you can choke on that stuff. So here I stand sopping, bedraggled in an old arcade speared through with wrought iron. The once blinking, flashhappy screens breathing dust and fiberglass. Motes shift and settle again like phantoms and I wait for the dark clouds to scatter and part. Watch clocks waltzing across the walls and shadows slowdancing.

Rain feels cleansing but it isn't. Nothing ever gets cleansed. We wear dirt on the inside where nothing blooms. Nothing pretty, at the very least.

Weeds, ivies, cockleburs.

To pass the hour, I hotwire a claw machine. Drop in an imaginary token, judge my depths from all sides, dangle the limp plastic talon over my prize and then end up smashing through the front with a balled-up bare fist because nothing matters anymore.

The teddy bear I take is badly faded, baby blue with a stitched-on smile and gross matted fur.

I brush off the flakes of glass, leave it sitting on the edge of one of the Skee-Ball lanes.

It's not mine to keep—I just couldn't bear to see it encased like that anymore.

All my defenses have been blown about by the powerful gale.

I'll have to replace them tomorrow, including every welcome pike.

I predict it will be a very busy (and messy) day.

Shooting a stare down through the grates, I watch my old friends scarfing down on a ripe body buffet. Beethoven appears to wink, but I warn myself this is likely just my imagination.

There is so much red down there. Syrupy, redolent, artificial almost. Ives stands neck deep in it, smacking sticky, the heap of meat slowly diminishing and in dire need of replenishment.

The wolves are just as startled as I am when we hear tiny voices chittering on the far side of the park.

*100 Kills*—that was the magic number on the battlefield.

Circulated among the battalion were unsubstantiated rumors that if you ever reached that mythical tally count, you'd get to walk free. The School of Fire, they called it, and those branded in it had earned their right to live on as an elder.

I never heard of anyone even getting close. Yet, there had to be someone, right? Aren't all myths rooted in some splinter of truth?

At a commendable tally of fifteen, I know exactly what kind of monster I am. But anything beyond that seems to transcend human.

A laugh here in Merrymouseland, these days, is as foreign sounding as an instrument. (Consider the Theremin and its high-pitched, ghostly whine—the only instrument I know of that doesn't actually require human contact with which to make music. Of this quirk I am insanely envious.) But a child's laugh in this place is even more surreal. Like a sunken chime tinkling across some far-flung, twilit abyss, it thoroughly confuses the ear, cutting through the rasping wind of an otherwise banal midmorning.

When I find its source, I also find four freckled faces squatting over a squirming rat.

Four ginger mops of hair with green grime-encrusted eyes, wearing drab olive uniforms missing several of their buttons.

*Youngers.*

I count two torn skirts and two tattered jackets with rounded collars. By the bright blue brands on their necks, I know right away from where they've come, as the initials 'JG' are synonymous with a life of diligent torment.

Josef Grimoire's dullhouse is infamous for its insidious efficacy. Never has an inheritor delighted so much in the playful persecution of his property. Twisted tales of what goes on behind the big brick walls vary from labyrinthine halls with hundreds of dead ends, Escheresque staircases, dizzying walls, barbwire pitfalls, and tessellated floors teased out with sharp visual illusions inviting escapees to tumble to their doom. In other words: mad scientist-type stuff.

Very few guards are required on the actual payroll, as the nightmarish architecture tends to take care of itself. (Perhaps some of these are grossly exaggerated but there's no way to know for sure. The only one I do suspect is 100% true, thanks to the manic ramblings of one of my fellow dethshepherds back in the day—a trustee who was eventually sold back to the youth battalion after a series of "unsuccessful nocturnal procedures," who claims to have been responsible for feeding the mewling *new bloods* for a short time—is that a quarter of its inhabitants are purchased at childbirth, bred and raised specifically to harvest their organs. According to that same source, this lot never knew they were among this lot, as such anonymity would be kept under lock and key. Another quarter of the children, known as the Chosen, would receive superior treatment with a certain modicum of luxury even: actual food, soft beds, sometimes even books to read. No one, not even this ex-trustee, would know for sure what separated the "spare parts" from the chosen, and neither would they. I imagine this ambiguity worked wonders to keep them all living in collective fear, constantly wondering whether they were being treated so well because their eventual health was only important for future resale value or whether Grimoire, in his false benevolence, had deemed that they are deserving of a better-quality life for some unknown, unknowable reason.

As for the remaining half, they were the ones who would tend to mount escapes, as they suffered endlessly, dead-eyed and cowlike with brains full of sloshing neurotoxins at night, when their daily food vitamin would get spat out into a dog bowl through large pneumatic rubber tubes just before bedtime. During the day, some might inevitably rise, wander the halls only to get lost. They would never make it back to the dog bowl for their lone capsule of sustenance and by then perhaps they wouldn't care.

I imagine them sometimes still, winding through the mazelike halls to Liszt's *Grand Galop Chromatique*. Out of breath. Out of options. Out of cares in the world.

Hope, I think, is a fixed, finite commodity—something you reach the end of just before diving.

Four voices blur together now as I press myself under a corrugated lip of tin, listening in.

"What's that? Who's there?"

"*Don't*, Miriam."

"I swear I heard something..."

"That's never a good thing."

"Maybe they have food!"

"Yeah! Maybe they're like us?"

"Get back over here. Both of you. NOW."

"I'm hungwy still."

"I know, Morrow. We all are."

"We'll find something. We always do."

[chomping] "More rat, I'm sure."

"Don't make fun, Sid. Food is food."

"....I'm sorry."

"It's ok. Miriam, come and eat some."


"After everyone else I will."

"You haven't had anything in a day. Please."

"Here, Mir. Take the rest of mine."

"Eat, silly. You're a growing young boy."

"I call the eyebaws!"

"You're such a strange child."

"That's enough. Eat. All of you. I'll watch."

"So cwunchy!"

"I'll take watch next. You need to eat too, Peter."

"I don't trust this place. We should move on."

"Not me! I like it."

"Me too! Merrymouse Merrymouse!"

As loud as they are, they won't make it through one more nightfall. And even if they are that lucky they'll likely attract every scabber across the Scorch.

This presents a problem for me – one of simple logistics.

I leave them to feast on their rodent kabob, for now, crossing the grate and asking the wolves what I should do.

*Red.*                           All I can see is red.

Compassion for animals is one thing—compassion for *human*animals is quite another.

Ultimately, it is a risk you can never afford.

Faraway, I can hear them laughing again. Skittering echoes bouncing into the beyond. Ping of pinballs.

I pretend I am a thing made of knives so as not to be palmed, crushed in the cave of a hand, pocketed or ravaged by its sprouting stalactites. Tell myself I am lemon-sulfur sun vomiting rays of furry needles. My anti-sunlight is shattering. Pestilential.

Devils may be lonely but at least they live on to spin their myths in the darkness.

If I had a forked tongue to flick in their direction, I would.

THINGS THE WAR OF SEVEN LAMBS TAUGHT ME:

In softness is death. In softness is death. In softness is death. In softness is death. Insoftness is death. In softness is death. In softness is death. In softness is death. In softness is death. In softness is death. In softness is death. In softness is death. In softness is death. In softness is death. In softness is death. In softness is death. In softness is

Snatches of wild grass poke up through rubble and I stomp over them, crushing all underfoot in my combat boots. Irises dripping icicles to ward off the petri and bacterium of this obsolete afterworld...

Come night, I'll count my bullets in peace (five tall: porcelain-painted, pretty as crackledile teeth... *Five*—that's one for each loudmouth and one left over, just in case...)

The youngers have settled on a crescent-shaped stage where an army of projectors once beamed down pinpricks of light to create a holographic midnight extravaganza. Even though it was the largest and most expensive production in Merrymouseland's roster of shows, it was the only one without any actual real actors. You'd think the parade, with all its ornate confetti-sloughing floats, ridiculous one-man bands, costumes and towering stilted jugglers, would take the cake but it turns out illusions are the most costly of all.

Night has arrived with a sudden chill, and they've been debating whether or not to start a fire for the last fifteen minutes. Peter, the eldest, thinks it's a bad move... it'll attract a bad element. His instinct is right but the littlest of the bunch, Morrow, has been putting on a maudlin show grinding her teeth. She has slowly begun to win him over along with her sister Miriam, who looks only slightly younger than Peter though she is nearing him in height, as she argues vociferously that warmth is indeed a necessity of survival.

The other boy, Sydney, the second youngest but biggest of all with a broad barrel chest, has been sitting still with his knees tucked up to his chest, waiting patiently for the argument to fold into his favor. He dares not speak out though, going against his brother. Somewhere, he picked up one of those dinky Merrymouse caps with a Technicolor propeller on top. It has been churning slowly for the last few minutes, his lips flapping a bit like a fish when the blustery winds blow.

I watch them through the greased black now, studying their features through my scope.

Where others would see only smudges I see fine details. They are thusly…

-Morrow has pigtails and two dimples punched into her cheeks framing a smile she has no business wearing in this ungodly place. She is carefree, happy, and will be the surefire death of the others because they would all die on the spot to protect her. Sometimes she sings to herself. She has been picking up rocks and other small, interesting pieces of trash all around the park and stealing them into her pockets when no one else is looking.

-Sydney has a bloated face, is naturally muscular and shuffles his feet whenever he walks. He seems disenthralled by every other thing that's happening, stutters sometimes when nervous, and has a habit of making piquant odd faces like a dinosaur whenever things get boring.

-Miriam has tresses like a waterfall on fire and sadness lives in her eyes, but she hides it well from the others, especially the little one who is constantly looking up to her or reaching out to snag her hand, which she does all the time. She is always there to take it.

-Finally, Peter the leader is no-nonsense with a grim symmetrical face. His hair always seems perfectly combed but his teeth never show. He is both the oldest and the youngest— perpetual panic dancing behind his eyelids, though he is quick to cool. He knows he must or else the others will see through him. He is the only one who really understands just how scared they should be.

In spite of this fact, he finally buckles. When he breaks down and finally builds a fire, I am disappointed in the part of him that knows he should know better.

*Pop!* go spastic embers as I slide Mausenstein back over my shoulders.

Dear Wolfmother,

Déja vu huh?

It could be so easy. Should be so easy.

I know what you'd say – I know I know... but you have to consider how clueless they are.

Not like your children, who had the inborn taste of blood in their system just waiting to be discovered. Secret palate yearning to be unlocked that lay dormant all their lives, like a room inside waiting for the right key to click.

That key, it turned out, was me, but I'm not sure I can be that same kind of key for them.

On the other hand, I suppose if they made it here AND survived a dullhouse they might have some kind of room inside them after all? Who knows. In time, maybe they'll learn what subtlety means. Either that or they'll be the death of both me and your furry progeny.

We'll find out I guess.

But if they do anything stupid like start a fire again, I'm calling the whole thing off.

Fair enough?

-C

Don't ever trust a composition that doesn't build from scratch. Doesn't earn its every crescendo. Everybody wants the big sounds right from the get-go – *to hell with tension!* says the impatient audience – but I prefer layers that build.

What fun is smashing a piano with a sledgehammer before you've even heard the harps herald, or those trumpets coughing deep through their brassy throats that something is terribly awry? In other words, I like music that lies to me. The only symphony worth hearing in this world is the one that pretends everything is going to be ok, and then proceeds to break your heart all at once.

## A BRIEF BULLETPOINT HISTORY OF THE MAN WHO STARTED IT ALL:

‣Mathison Mauswick Jr. was born to Mathison and Ethel Mauswick in Gildymare, Maine on December 4th, 1911

‣By all accounts he was a lonely child with social deficiencies that, for whatever reason, prevented him from making the kind of friends otherwise endowed by an idyllic childhood

‣I say idyllic, by which I mean he was never beaten but certainly scolded beyond reasonable measures for typical juvenile behaviors like talking to himself in the bathtub, climbing the big magnolia tree in the front yard, folding paper, or bouncing a rubber ball inside the house

‣He was slightly closer to his mother, who sang to him off-tune lullabies but only when he was already asleep. It was customary for his father, a naturally withdrawn figure, to offer him a handshake in lieu of hugs, which he deemed more than satisfactory to convey his paternal approval

‣Mathison did poorly in school but enjoyed art. He had many bullies. His early journals were filled with whimsical doodles which included formative sketches of all the classic Merrymouse© characters that would eventually bring him fame, recognition, and longlasting success

‣"Mathy," as he was called by his secretary, premiered his first full-length feature, *Pip Piper the Faunboy*, at the tender age of 22. It was an instant hit, filling its young wide-eyed debut audience, whom he bussed in to see it for free, with the kind of effervescent wonder that his brand would be known for generations later

‣Mathy never married nor did he engage in any traditional courting rituals during adolescence

‣Mathy was not ugly even though he felt ugly all his life, which might as well be the same thing

‣Consider a child so starved for conventional friendship that he resorts to drawing more unconventional friends into being. These are not humans but animals—silly apocryphal playmates bounding across the neatly compressed void of a white abyss, made kinetic, suddenly brought to life with the shuffle of a page and the bright blood of his ink

▸Consider a child pressing his precious drawings to his chest in a silent basement, weeping just out of the sunlight slicing through the window because he much prefers mute, lopsided shadows over the blinding knives of sunlight's symmetry

▸Consider the sadness that spirals down

▸Consider all the events in-between…a rise, a fall

▸Consider an old man on his deathbed, still pressing his precious drawings to his chest— the crumpled Rosebuds of what he, though nobody else, would deem a ruinous career

▸Consider all the joy invented by such secret loneliness

▸Consider the heart as a delicate, stringed instrument—how it can be plucked as easily as it can be broken

Through the night-pigment, I shuffle back down to where the laughing idiots lay sprawled. Defenseless, without even a makeshift tent to camouflage their twitching bodies.

Sydney is snoring loudly as Morrow sleeps like no human I've ever seen: her birdlike body contorting into impossible positions that lead me to believe she might be missing some bones. Miriam has one arm draped over the little one, as if cradling her dreams, while Peter is seconds from accidentally rolling off the stage. I am certain he fell asleep attempting to sit upright on the edge, trying to keep guard and doing a terrible job of it.

It is then I spot a familiar silhouette lurching, sharing the same darkness I am, with the same plan in mind no doubt. I am startled but not surprised. He is grown, hungry, and up to his own tricks again.

*Nuh uh*, I shake my head softly at Ives to let him know: if they're going to be anybody's they're going to be mine. Eventually he backs off, and I am left watching the idiots alone again.

I let my blade, which has grown brittle, slip back into its sheath slowly.

It won't kill me to spare them another day, I suppose?

"4'33" is a three-movement composition by American composer John Cage. It consists of four minutes, thirty-three seconds of silence and whatever sound the audience happens to make during the duration of its performance.

As such, for three minutes and thirty-three seconds, the following human tics, gestures, and utterances are magically metamorphosed into incantatory music: heavy breaths, coughs, sneezes, sighs, slurps, belches, farts, yawns, scratches, nose-picks, hair-slicks, scalp-rubs, knuckle-crunches, neck cracks, chair squeaks, change-jingles, teeth grinding, picking of scabs, pulling of cuticles, exasperated sputtering, manic fidgeting, gasps, guffaws, lips smacking, slow-pleading smiles, muffled sobs, the occasional rhapsodic scream, and dubious, unrelentingly-slow crinkling of assorted candies and various provisions culled from the bottom of some oversized, antediluvian purse like a fistful of shiny doubloons wrested up from an ancient seabed.

Bony birds shriek as the Norman Rockwell sun pistons up into a pumpernickel sky.

Suddenly, they are gone. As in abracadabra, presto, alla kazam. Nowhere to be found in The Golden Kingdom among the muck-encrusted marionettes, who have ceased to sing their grating song due to the wild wisteria and bougainvillea tumbling overgrown out of their throats in great clots, tufts and tangles. Nor in any of the overpriced eateries of Zinny Yuh's *Neigh*borhood, or the collapsed attraction booths of Dafty Dill's Kiddy Corner, with its scads of deflated midway balloons or smashed grand prize goldfish bowls.

Even the stage where they once slept offers no signs of a fire.

I stroll through the park, on my own again, darting eyes and scanning the blighted horizon. Pass the grate to hear the grown wolves savagely sneering.

I honestly can't tell anymore if its hunger or loneliness.

Somewhere deep in the twisty bowels of Manic Mangoose's Monstery Manor, I sail adrift on a headless swan. Civilization dances upon the edge of a knife as my wafer-thin raft toggles half a lonely headlight over phalanxes of the incandescent dead.

In the center of a labyrinth, upon witnessing a flock of phantoms through warped remnants of a shattered mirror, I find my own reflection has gone suspiciously amiss. Whinny screams in a dusk-colored sadness twirling in the center of the room as trick projectors twitch.

Faithless apparitions bound by their bodily exodus.

It is not until later, when I am standing in the empty gallery of the Hall of Obscure Dignitaries sans a single dignitary, that I really begin to worry.

Dear Wolfmother,

How do you tell if you're losing your mind?

-C

I once saw the ocean – the real ocean – back before the world went the way of bleached bone. Its cutting tides were like blueblack glass, curlicue crests bouncing along frothy spines of white and percussive waves crashing.

Spinning gulls would be overhead wheeling figure 8s. All the half-buried critters below, their pincers perched along the nape where land's edge blurred into a mystic, deadly undertow.

Sanity too, I think, is some kind of terrible ocean.

Everything erodes eventually.

Everything erodes eventual.

Everything erodes event.

Everything erodes even.

Everything erodes.

Everything ero.

Everything er.

Everything.

Every.

Ever.

Eve.

E.

According to Mousekipedia, the official Merrymouse Wiki, there's a secret apartment where Mathison Mauswick Jr. used to stay whenever he visited the premises. There, it is said he sketched quietly in the corner, eating saltless and pepperless hard-boiled eggs with sugarless black coffee, listening to old opera records. There were no windows in this suite, as per his request, though allegedly the walls were thinly constructed so he could hear the uproarious laughter of all the joy he brought about in his fans. Just a drab little space fit for a lonely king.

One unconfirmed trivia tidbit (and you won't find this anywhere on the Wiki): he fooled around with stop motion a bit just before his death, even going so far as to film an entire experimental short in his bedroom, which it is said he hated. Most dispute this, citing his hate of the technology.

Anyway, this apartment was the first place I sought out when I found my way here, but when I finally found it I couldn't bring even myself to cross the threshold.

♪ Currently playing, ♪ when I finally hear their high-flung, familiar voices near the west gate: *Literally any nocturne by Frédéric François Chopin.*

Such sweet confirmation it is I'm not just inventing a parade of faces to occupy my waning mind, that I rush to glimpse them through the Doric scaffolding. There, on the other side, I see they are hunting for bogfruit and other slimy succulents knee-deep in the swamps.

Given that they're no doubt unaware of the meat-lusting ivory gluttons native to this area, in which they're cluelessly frolicking, suddenly I can sense my own nerves caroming and gamboling about underneath my skin. Then, when I see how they've noosed the cord around the smallest one's waist, urging her only deeper into the depths, my nerves prick up — stiff-necked as a gazelle having just heard a rustle at the top of the hill.

"Be careful, Mor."

"Got one! Eww, slimy."

"I can already taste it!"

"They look kinda disgusting."

"Easy does it now..."

As she comes up with a fistful of blooming umbrellas I'm already bolting, heel-locked for the tunnels with a plan to win them away from their watery deaths.

The Fantastic Idiots, I think I'll call them for now on.

I am surprised to find the ringer to Mauswick's Memorial Bell exactly where I left it—nestled in oily rags, under a pile of canned goods collecting dust in E5, where even a grimer would be hard-pressed to find it.

Once again it is Beethoven who spares me when I have no choice but to cross the wolves in the corridor, sledding past with my potted meat and spilling vegetables piled high. Though he is considerably lacking in what warmth I remember, his once-puny face grown long and grizzled. Eyes much sadder now. Sparkless, only half willing to rise and greet mine.

I am glazed in sweat by the time I strike the bell, hear it peel out through the park like water insidiously spreading. It is the only thing loud enough to lure them away from their death-inviting hijinks. Before they find my grimy tower of cans awaiting them at the west gate, though – a feast fit for miniature kings – I'll watch those albino bumps in the water beginning to circle them.

They'll never know how close to the end they were...as I'll never know why I stopped them, when their presence here could only mean one thing: a bloody and calamitous fate for us all, the few and luckless still-living.

You won't be the first person in the history of existence to reap disappointment at the crushing discovery that, despite all of your carefully orchestrated efforts, you still need other people.

Dear Wolfmother,

Today the air was alkaline and I found myself gasping to breathe. I raked off Mausenstein and found another spritz of silver in my hair. Immediately cut it off and launched a gob of green phlegm over the artificial canyon in Daydream Springs—a series of lateral geysers embedded under brown astroturf that would spurt just over children's heads on a hot day, allowing parents a brief respite from their hand-holding and crowd-cruising. I imagined the peop...the *youngers* I mean, as rats flooding through the valley, cheeks fat with candy.

When I snuck back into the tunnels to liberate what rations I could from my cache, on my way out Ives gave chase and this time Beethoven didn't stop him. I watched the alpha literally snubbing his snout in my direction as his brother kicked up trash, flitting through the void. I lost a boot; its sole is presently tooth-snagged at the entrance where it will remain. I confess: I barely escaped intact in my own skin. I'm not mad, nor disappointed, or even surprised; everything defaults back to the way of Nature's Knife eventually.

In my next life, remind me to will myself into a wolf, but for now I'm stuck in this clammy humansuit.

What to do with my fellow clumsy humansuits, though?

What to do, what to do.

If you can spare it, do send me some guidance.

Be well.

-C

"Don't, Mor. It could be a trap."

"But it's food!"

"It could be poisoned."

"But, food!!!"

"Morrow, I said no."

"But, food?"

"But who put it here?"

"F O O D."

"And Why? Think."

"It does look better than mushrooms though."

"There she goes."

"No, Morrow, don't!"

I watch Peter attempt to tear her away from the pyramid of cans as she bites him; watch him wagging his arm, wincing away the sight of blood. She grabs a can and smashes it down on the concrete. The others watch her a moment, licking their lips then feasting on the splatter of cranberries, until they decide to join her, dipping their hands in and sopping up the canned treat. Soon they're all three smashing cans together.

Only Peter is resisting the impulse. "Fine!" His arm continues to drip as he's daubing it on his sleeve. "But if you all die I get to say I told you so." Then he's looking up and around, painfully aware whoever placed the pile there is likely watching them now at this very moment.

I press my body flat behind a crumpled Port-a-Potty.

"Just don't eat it all," he amends wisely, giving in. "Save some. We have to live beyond just today, you know."

Later that same day, I watch them playing house. I sit here, eating a fistful of beetles. Rolling their mushy carapaces across my molars, grown soft in the acidic earth.

Miriam folds a large tarp like fresh laundry while Sydney draws widening spirals over the sidewalk. Morrow is snoring inside a hollowed-out plastic rocket while Peter adds the finishing touches to their domicile for the night—a standard tinfoil teepee.

For the better part of three hours Peter has been closely monitoring them for signs of poisoning. ("How's your stomach?" "Tell me if it hurts." "Vomit if you feel even the least bit funny!" "I swear if you all die I'm going to kill you for leaving me alone.") Even this, he wouldn't dare enact. I can feel his fear of aloneness vibrating all the way from here.

Then, an hour later, as Sydney sits shaking a tourniquet of bees and Miriam crafts lavender giraffes from resort soap, I can still feel Peter's fatal flaw prickling as he wanders past me, seeking out something elsewhere in the park. I'm just about to hop down from the stump where I've squatted unseen when a tiny, melancholic voice sneaks up behind me.

"Hello," says Morrow, addressing me somewhat spookily. It is the first time anyone has ever snuck up on me. Thankfully, my mask is secure; armor snapped on implacably tight.

You would think it would be enough to scare her off.

You would be wrong.

Mathison Mauswick Jr. always secretly dreamed of fame. More subdued, perhaps, than the narcissistic ego-greed of someone patently ridiculous like Lord Mudpant, it was always dormant nonetheless—a persistent longing for that which could only be found outside the self, with its too-many corners, manifolds, shadow-shot furrows.

A talented grimer, out here in the Scorch, can still find some semblance of fame, that for which I have no desire.

But at times a wheedling voice comes to haunt you in the dark slate of your skull: the fear your name will die in a blender of oblivion with neither dent nor din... That you have been marked unremarkable—an obscure footnote relegated to the afterpages of some book that no one even bothered to write...        That you are a minor comet, whistling futily through history's nameless aether... You are haunted by the irrepressible suspicion you deserve all the evils this decadent, red world has wrought and that you are, when all the crucial figures get carried over, remainders landing with thudding finality, exactly as ugly and invisible as you feel.

A SHORT HISTORY OF HUMAN BEINGS: a legacy of chasing love at every corner with often disastrous results. And, if failing to find it, chasing hate instead. If not the hate of others any sharply made mirror.

"I'm nobody," I speak down to the youngest of the youngers now, realizing it is no lie. To my chagrin, she persists.

"Everybody's somebody." She pitches her shoulders, pointing west to the wall, where CODA has been blowtorched. One of my first and most permanent creations, not too long ago when the world seemed too loud and I sat shrinking into myself.

A parachuting breeze passes over us now, carrying with it a molding-ammonia pungency and I imagine briny kelp growing out of my skin. It is at that moment I decide she could be the alpha. That she will be the next alpha...she just doesn't know it yet.

"It's safer to be nobody." I nod to her, trying to take my leave but turn only to find her eldest sister in my path.

"Thank you," she squeaks out, looking starstruck. "For the food, I mean."

I navigate my way around her only to find another idiot smackdab in my path now, his dumb propeller cap twirling. He smiles, showing off bright pink gums with a makeshift giraffe in his giant, outstretched open palm. "I'm Sydney. You can call me Syd though. That's easier to say."

I start to say something sarcastic but worry he might confuse it for encouragement, so instead say nothing, choosing a third direction away from all three.

"Help us," the eldest sister pleads, trying to keep pace as the other two shuffle after her.

Suddenly I'm ensnared.

"Please?"

Now I'm definitely sure: it was a mistake to lead them along. To offer them even one morsel let alone hope for survival. Anybody who would dare ask for help doesn't deserve the amenities of living, even in the pickled shitslums of this dust zoo. I walk faster.

"At least give us some tips!" Miriam boldly decrees, flustered. "We deserve that much."

Tips. As if one could learn the indelicate skills of survival needed in this mausoleum of mucus. Fair enough.

I flash three fingers, then mime the first of the tips by tapping my sword and thumping my rifle. "Learn how to use them." Jam two fingers together for the second tip and slash my lips, indicating the sacredness of silence and its potential usefulness in keeping them attached to their skin longer. Lastly, I wave three fingers in front of the youngest's face. "Follow her instead. That other one'll get you killed."

About that time Peter presents himself, looking upon me with holy disdain.

"Get away from him," he commands the others.

"Her!" Morrow is quick to correct him.

"Get away from her," he tries again, slowly placing himself between us.

I can tell by the look on his face he's seen some of my work. I just don't know what yet.

"It's OK, Peter! She's gonna help us! She"

"—NOW," he tugs at Morrow, looking upon me as if I'm the angel of death. I am.

"There's bodies. What's left of them, anyway. Mostly bones. In a pit."

Ah huhhh.

Morrow is the only one who seems the least bit concerned about this newest revelation, smiling up at me still. "They were all bad I bet," she is so sure. "Right, Coda?!"

Red. All I can see is red. Rush of fur. Gleeful glint of snarling fang through the darkness of the tunnels. An opus of memory.

It is times like this I remember what I am. Mausenstein more fitting than my real face: some stitched-on smile worn by a monster beyond repair.

"Right," I ensure her in a dead monotone.

Then I am stepping, roving automaton under scrabble of dusk; a hay-thick midmorning glower. I am gone. And they, they are left bickering just as loudly as they were the moment my mind airbrushed them into existence.

*Dear Wolfmother,*

*Could you feel the end coming before it did? Was it like frail electricity—an insouciant voltage? And if you could, did it make it any easier to endure or did it make it worse?*

*I wonder. Because humans, they live the whole of their lives knowing it's coming – that it's inevitable - yet how they excel at pretending otherwise. Maybe it's a necessary evil, this charade? Maybe that's all this life is in the end—little games we concoct until the timer runs out. Sand sifting through some invisible hourglass.*

*I only ask because sometimes I think I feel it coming too: The End. Like voids that swallow themselves, one impinging endlessly into the next.*

*And I shrivel and shrink at the sight of it, because I know I am not nearly as brave as you.*

*My teeth are too brittle. Instincts too dull. I am not fast enough to endure, nor am I strong enough to die with even a quarter of your sacrifice.*

*I have never feared death, not since the war, but I fear it now.*

*And I can feel the sand tumbling away. Galloping us all, we pitiful living, toward the cliffs of our impending hour to be swallowed whole by our hate.*

*-C*

Come night, I count my bullets in peace. Five tall, porcelain-painted, pretty as crackledile teeth. Crooked under that terrifically realistic harpoon hung in the pirate's eye, I watch them down below still—my flock of fantastic idiots. Packing slowly, hurling what little provisions they can muster into polka-dotted hobo sacks they'll soon cinch onto the ends of sticks. They'll bump along over the horizon like rags of ghosts – shadows sewn into their skin sulking toward the  swirling trash ocean. Grit-knuckled and gnarled, at least they'll be safe from me then.

For all Peter's faults, he can sense a bad apple. The vile worm wriggling, rotting inside its softening core.

They'll last no longer than a day in the open scorch; this is an optimistic estimate.

But of course, it is still within my powers to spare them and this crosses my mind more than once. (Five tall, porcelain-painted, pretty as crackledile teeth...) I watch dazed birds – or maybe they're bats and I could never tell the difference? – pirouetting like little cocktail umbrellas over the greased night's canvas.

I have decided I have no idea what mercy is, and even if I did I'm not worthy of doling it out. So I'll do nothing. Simply, *nothing.*    What a relief—to be unmoored from fate like that. A passive observer, no more, no less.

It's easier that way; I'm starting to believe the trick is to let things go by and not try to

catch them at all. Call me driftwood. Watch me float.

As the plink of rain settles in, splashing off the cragged lips of my tower, Maurice Ravel's ♪ *Pavane for Dead Princess* ♪ washes over me and I spy the youngers stirring. Frantic mumbling beneath a pre-wintry spritz, racing for cover from the elements.

Morrow is watching me, though I know am safe here ringed in this dark socket. If not for her – that squinched face of confusion, the essence of innocence radiating over many miles – I would have already deleted them. Swept them from my memory like a knocked-over chessboard, but there they remain, as real as ever, and as she is locked on the board I am locked too, and so I happen to notice the grim silhouette bending through the rain toward them.

Tall and wiry and cloaked in gashlets of silver fog, it appears as some hateful scarecrow lurching up from the fields. Uncrucified from its post and come alive with a vengeance for all crows.

It is his face that emerges first—crowned in chaotic circles, spiral upon unholy spiral. Blinkless. Mouthless. Horrifying.

A grimer...and he has come for them. Come for us all.

All my synapses fire yet I remain frozen.

TO BE CONTINUED...
DEAR WOLFMOTHER
Parts III & IV [SCHERZO///WINTER + SONATA///
SPRING]
To Be Concluded In:
CENTRIPEDAL: COUNTER-STORIES

Matthew Burnside

Centrifugal

# AN ANNOTATED TRANSCRIPT OF DR. DIGBY BRADFORD-MORROW'S GRADUATE CREATIVE WRITING WORKSHOP OF ALFRED HITCHCOCK'S THE BIRDS

"Title is a little too on the nose. What if you dropped The, so it's just: BIRDS (?)"

"I get the concept of the birds. I like it, think it works, is clever. However, there are just so many birds. I have to ask, are all these birds earned?"

"There were so many liminal spaces in this story, liminally-speaking, I mean. I wonder if there could be even more liminal spaces? Maybe I'm just a fan of saying the word liminal, though."

"Why birds? Why not geckos, or ponies?"

"Really well written! I have to confess it was nearly impossible for me to tell each bird apart though. Why not give them names? Or maybe just more particularity of details? Little hats, perhaps, all different kinds...to make it easier for the reader to differentiate each individual bird, you know?"

"On that same note, I found it very difficult to relate to the birds. I wonder if you could interweave flashbacks to help us relate to their struggle, because I really wanted to invest in them as characters and better understand their motivation as birds."

"I don't get the ending. Or the beginning. Or middle."

"I would've liked to see more kinds of birds: parrots, for example. Or a toucan that talks for comic relief, maybe. Some flamingos, I dunno."

"This has nothing to do with the story but if I ever invent my own candy I'll probably call them Liminems."

"Maybe it's just me but I wanted this to be much more erotic than it turned out to be. The birds didn't even fuck once and I really think that was a missed opportunity on the part of the author."

"What about a revisionist retelling? Flip that shit—what if the humans attacked the birds?"

"I feel like I was reading a completely different story than all you guys?"

"Like, a shitload of birds. What if it was just one big bird?"

"This was my favorite piece that I've read in the course all year. Having said that, it was also my least favorite piece."

"Hey guys, I figured it out! I read the wrong story."

"I didn't get a chance to read all of this one yet, I'll be honest, but having scanned it just these last few minutes I will say my favorite scene is probably the one with the birds."

"I like the idea but in the end it just doesn't seem realistic to me. In real life, birds don't act like that."

"Liminal."

Matthew Burnside

Centrifugal

# ENCORE

## Act I

Here's the thing—the clown isn't laughing. He's just sitting there on his stool in the center of the tent, sharpening his banana into a knife. This is after twisting together a balloon elephant and making my sister cry, popping it with a pin hidden between his teeth.

Just a balloon, Dad said, cracking a peanut. All a part of the show, kiddo. Just watch!

Dad knows best; he wouldn't bring us to something that would disappoint us. Eat some more cotton candy, he says.

I do.

## Act II

Who wants to fly? The clown is asking now as trapezists powder their hands. Where's the net?

A few giddy volunteers are hoisted up. They go swinging, slung, caught by their ankles. One slips, doesn't quite make it. A dull thud as lights go out. Clowns dance through the dark smeared in glowing make up, sleepy organ cranking while somebody cleans up the mess with a mop, leaving a puddle of mush in the middle. Weeping mother is ushered backstage by the ringleader. He removes his tall hat out of respect for her sacrifice, all in service of the show. His twisty mustache doesn't flinch.

Now who wants to come down and put their head in the lion's mouth? the clown says.

This time no one is volunteering. Eventually, a father convinces his son to not be chicken. Go on boy, give em a show!

Dads know best; they wouldn't let the lion hurt us.

When the child, hands in pocket, places his head in the lion's mouth he is nervously laughing. Because what else can you do with your head in a lion's mouth?

Clown with banana knife gives the crowd a wink.

Everyone woos, wahs.

When the big cat's jaw snaps it looks fake. Nameless boy's body with neck nub makes no sound as it falls. Then there are trumpets and tubas and confetti in the air.

What a spectacle eh kiddo? Dad spits out a shell. I honestly don't understand how they did that last trick but everyone is already clapping, so I put my hands together awkwardly. My stomach hurts, tied in triple knots.

Act III

Time for the finale! proclaims the ringleader, back in action. He snaps and they roll out a cannon.

How many kids do you think we can cram inside? he wants to know.

I hold my sister's hand to let her know I'm here. I see it, too.

Other parents are pushing their kids forward now, urging them to climb the ladder and crawl into the cannon's hissing mouth. They do even though it's scary and most of them are crying.

When the man with the tall hat and inflexible mustache lights it a tongue of flame goes licking across the ring, spattering flaps red with specks, black powder residue, and little bits of bone and teeth. Then a spark catches the cloth, goes crawling along the tent's skin.

Dad will know what to do; he wouldn't let any of this happen.

When I turn to him, he's sucking down a peanut. How many people do you know personally who have been murdered by a clown? he puts it to me as I watch people behind him bleeding, stabbed by a murderous clown with a banana knife. They sag, slip down in the cracks like deflated balloons.

Me personally? Well, zero.

There ya go! Dad smiles. Don't be ridiculous.

Act IV

The tent is burning down from the inside. We watch the head clown crawl into his tiny car with ten of his friends and zip away. Its little engine sputters along, tailpipe hiccupping exhaust. A bloody banana peel splashes down in a puddle in front of us, flung out the window.

Before I take my sister out I say goodbye to our parents.

Bye, Dad.

Bye, kiddo.

His eyes are gone. A blankness: glassed-over sheen of swimmy blue. There is nothing there.

Wave goodbye forever, I tell my sister. Her shoulders scrunch.

We watch the tent burning from a safe distance. Smoke curling, poles collapsing. Sky red as a loon's eye. Mom and Dad sat smiling somewhere still inside. We can hear their hands on fire, clapping through the burning.

Bravo, Bravo! What a show.

Tomorrow there shall be another.

219

Centrifugal

# LITTLE GOD THINGS

Why do anything? Why left? Why not right? Why this versus that? Why war? Why peace? Why love? Why hate? Why diffidence? Why violence? Why bombs? Why doves? Why graves? Why weeping mother? Why solemn father? Why country? Why flag? Why religion? Why pulpit? Why pew? Why feel? Why drugs? Why neurons? Why weary? Why sleep? Why dream? Why eat? Why drink? Why all appetites beyond hunger? Why bodies? Why appendages? Why tongues? Why words? Why not just pictures? Why ghosts? Why haunt? Why not robots? Why not lasers? Why teeth? Why not fangs? Why moonglow? Why sunsick? Why trees? Why rocks? Why leaves? Why waves? Why wolves?

Why howl?

Why little marks on paper?

Why write a story?

Why tell it like that?

Why not funnier?

Why not more serious?

Why read it?

Why lie?

Why truth?

Why if?

Why ever?

Why never?

Why not?

## About the Author

Matthew Burnside is a nice guy.

## About the Publisher

Whisk(e)y Tit is committed to restoring degradation and degeneracy to the literary arts. We work with authors who are unwilling to sacrifice intellectual rigor, unrelenting playfulness, and visual beauty in our literary pursuits, often leading to texts that would otherwise be abandoned in today's largely homogenized literary landscape. In a world governed by idiocy, our commitment to these principles is an act of civil service and civil disobedience alike.